Careless

CARRIE ANN RYAN

NEW YORK TIMES BESTSELLING AUTHOR

CARELESS
AN ASHFORD CREEK PREQUEL

CARRIE ANN RYAN

PRAISE FOR CARRIE ANN RYAN

"Count on Carrie Ann Ryan for emotional, sexy, character driven stories that capture your heart!" – Carly Phillips, NY Times bestselling author

"Carrie Ann Ryan's romances are my newest addiction! The emotion in her books captures me from the very beginning. The hope and healing hold me close until the end. These love stories will simply sweep you away." ~ NYT Bestselling Author Deveny Perry

"Carrie Ann Ryan writes the perfect balance of sweet and heat ensuring every story feeds the soul." - Audrey Carlan, #1 New York Times Bestselling Author

"Carrie Ann Ryan never fails to draw readers in with passion, raw sensuality, and characters that pop off the page. Any book by Carrie Ann is an absolute treat." – New York Times Bestselling Author J. Kenner

"Carrie Ann Ryan knows how to pull your heartstrings and make your pulse pound! Her wonderful Redwood Pack series will draw you in and keep you reading long into the night. I can't wait to see what comes next with the new generation, the Talons. Keep them coming, Carrie Ann!" –Lara Adrian, New York Times bestselling author of CRAVE THE NIGHT

"With snarky humor, sizzling love scenes, and brilliant, imaginative worldbuilding, The Dante's Circle series reads as if Carrie Ann Ryan peeked at my personal wish list!" – NYT Bestselling Author, Larissa Ione

"Carrie Ann Ryan writes sexy shifters in a world full of passionate happily-ever-afters." – *New York Times* Bestselling Author Vivian Arend

"Carrie Ann's books are sexy with characters you can't help but love from page one. They are heat and heart blended to perfection." *New York Times* Bestselling Author Jayne Rylon

Carrie Ann Ryan's books are wickedly funny and deliciously hot, with plenty of twists to keep you guessing. They'll keep you up all night!" USA Today Bestselling Author Cari Quinn

"Once again, Carrie Ann Ryan knocks the Dante's Circle series out of the park. The queen of hot, sexy, enthralling paranormal romance, Carrie Ann is an author not to miss!" *New York Times* bestselling Author Marie Harte

CARELESS

An Ashford Creek Prequel

CHAPTER 1

Felicity

"**H**appy birthday!"

I grinned at my four friends who I'd dragged up to my small town from college. The crew not only knew how to plan an event, but they were also a fearsome foursome of joy, exuberance, and abundance.

Lauren, Laura, Laurelin, and Laurel had been best friends since grade school. They'd all lived in the same suburb of Denver, gone to the same schools, lived within the same group of neighborhoods—even though they'd moved a couple of times throughout their lives—and went to Denver State University. They'd split dorm rooms, and when it had come to renting a house for their junior and senior years, they'd all lived together. And somehow, I had been enveloped in their L-named arms when I'd been on the hunt for an off-campus room.

Sadly, as my parents had named me Felicity, and I didn't quite fit in name-wise—or in many aspects otherwise—but I loved these girls. They treated me nicely and reminded me I wasn't alone even though I was technically a small-town girl, complete with Journey's musical lyrics.

"Thank you!" I said as we each held up our shot glass of tequila, tapped it on the bar top, and slugged it back.

The burn was like nothing else I'd had in my life. It felt as if a clawed hand scraped down my throat, set it on fire, and told me *that trash* was the most amazing and delicate taste that would send me over the edge.

I choked, throat burning, before I bit into the lime that Laura handed me.

"You were supposed to lick the salt first, silly," Laurelin teased.

Eyes watering, I blinked a few times and set the shot glass down on the bar top. The bartender with familiar eyes just raised a brow at me, and I ignored him.

Of course, I was going to ignore him tonight.

Rune would never let me hear the end of it. After all, he was my big brother. At least one of them. In a world of over-protectiveness, I had two big brothers. While Atlas was out on the road, playing for the Portland Gliders and kicking ass as a goalie in the NHL, Rune had stayed behind in our small town of Ashford Creek because he loved the place. Or so he said.

And I stood here in Summit Grill, his bar and grill—the only true one in all of Ashford Creek—and nodded in thanks as he handed over a glass of water.

"Oh, thank you," Laurel purred as she fluttered her eyelashes at my big brother.

I gagged again, but this time, it wasn't over the drinks. "Hey, remember what I said. No hitting on my brother," I said with a laugh and choked once again since the burn of tequila wouldn't go away. "How do people drink this?" I asked before chugging half of my water.

It was my twenty-first birthday tonight, and

while I was going to drink to my heart's content because that's just what you did and I didn't mind following some traditions, I wasn't going to be an idiot and end up with alcohol poisoning. Hence why I knew exactly how many drinks I was going to have. I marked each shot or cocktail with a Sharpie on my arm and was required to have one glass of water per drink.

The four Ls didn't follow my mantra, but Rune wouldn't serve me in his bar if I didn't. And while he was grumpy, kind of mean, and way too overprotective, he was right.

"Oh, I forgot he was your brother," Laurel said with a soft laugh, still fluttering those eyelashes. She was probably going to blink out her contacts soon if she didn't stop.

"There's my baby girl."

Head slightly spinning, chest warm, and throat finally hydrated, I looked over and held back a groan—even though a smile crept over my face.

Gwen Carter, with all her gorgeous honey-blonde hair, threw herself at me and hugged me tightly. Jackson Carter followed behind and picked us both up as if we weighed nothing and as if the man wasn't in his fifties.

"Mom. Dad. You're here!" I quickly glanced

down at my arm, grateful I was only on drink two of the night. Dad set us both down and kissed the top of my head. I didn't miss the look, that glance between the four Ls. Maybe they weren't as close to their parents, but I was. I loved them. I wasn't exactly embarrassed by them.

"I didn't know you guys were going to be here tonight," I said, and didn't miss the rough chuckle Rune gave from behind the bar.

"Like these two would miss their baby girl out in the world, able to drink legally. When their son owns this bar? No. I don't know why you're surprised."

I barely resisted the temptation to flip him off. It didn't matter that I was now twenty-one—my parents would kick my butt if I flipped him off or cursed at him. I may be an adult who was now two legal drinks into my night, but I was still the baby girl, and there were rules in Ashford Creek.

I put on a bright smile, hoping the cracks didn't show at the edges, and gestured to the four Ls. "Mom, Dad, this is Lauren, Laura, Laurelin, and Laura."

"It's so nice to meet you," my mom said as she leaned forward and hugged each and every one of them.

They hugged her back, looking surprised, and yet each melted into my mother's embrace. That was my mom—sweet, slightly terrifying if somebody hurt one of her cubs, and the mom's mom. After all, I knew that each of my friends had their own mother issues, but I actually liked my parents.

Shocking.

"The next round is on us," my dad said as he gestured towards Rune.

"You don't have to do that, Dad," I said as I wrapped my arm around his waist.

"Just one because I'm old, and I'm joining you guys."

"Every time you call yourself old, you're calling me old, darling, as we're the same age," Mom teased.

"No, no, you stopped aging at twenty-eight. I know the rules."

I smiled at their banter as they kept going, and Rune made a round of drinks for everyone. This time, not tequila.

"And water for you," Rune said as he gestured towards my second glass.

"Of course. Thank you, everybody," I said as we each clinked glasses and, this time, slowly sipped our drinks.

The music blared a country tune that was easy to dance to, and by drink four, my parents were gone, Rune wasn't behind the bar anymore, as he owned the place, so he didn't always have to work there, and the four Ls and I were on the dance floor, trying to pick up the line-dancing moves.

"How are you so good at this?" Lauren asked with a little annoyance in her tone.

"I don't know. I just follow what the person in front of me is doing," I said, gesturing to the gorgeous redhead in front of me. I didn't know her name, and that surprised me. Ashford Creek wasn't exactly a tourist town. Yes, people came up here and stayed during the summer months, as well as stayed here if they wanted to ski at the resort a little bit away. We were cheaper than the major resort town next door, and that meant they could save money and only had to deal with a drive that, thankfully, the town had leaned into. We had a bus line, an entire community line of vehicles to get people to that tourist destination.

But on a Wednesday night at my brother's place, I wasn't used to seeing strangers.

Then again, I hadn't been home in a while.

I came for the holidays, of course, but it was few and far between because I still worked down in

Denver. My parents and Rune came to visit often, as did Atlas when he wasn't on the road. Hockey season was always weird to me because even when he wasn't playing, he was still training and conditioning. My brother worked harder than anybody I knew, and I was sad that he couldn't be here.

Just then, Laurelin sucked in a breath, and the hairs on the back of my neck stood on end.

I turned, and there he was.

The man of my dreams. *My hero.*

I held back a snort at that.

Callum Ashford wasn't my hero. Okay, maybe he was. He had been a teenager when I had been a little younger, as I was an 'oops' baby, and he'd saved me after I'd fallen off my bike.

He'd put the Band-Aid on my knee, kissed the top of it, and told me I was going to be okay.

All I had to do was smile and let others I could trust know I was hurting, and they would take care of it. But I wasn't a little girl anymore, and Callum had grown into those wide shoulders of his.

"Oh my God, you did not tell me that Ashford Creek made men like that," Laura whispered.

"They sure do," I mumbled.

"Between your brother and whoever that bearded man is, I am in love."

Jealousy zinged up my spine, but I told myself it was fine. I wasn't going to act on it. Callum knew who I was, of course. Because I was Rune and Atlas's little sister. Although I hadn't truly seen him in years. He'd left town when he was seventeen and come back to town right when I had left for college. So I had known him when we'd both been kids, and now we were both adults, and he looked far better than any dream I had made up of him.

"Ashford," an old man called out, and Callum raised a brow.

"Are you talking to me or one of the other Ashfords?" he asked dryly.

"Wait, is his name the same as the town? Is his family royalty or something?" Laurelin whispered, slightly tipsy on her feet.

I handed her my water, but she ignored it, going for her vodka Red Bull.

Shrugging, I chugged the rest of my water and picked up my own vodka Red Bull. This was drink five. Or six. Had I labeled that on my arm? I was fine. Right? Oh no. Time for more water.

"The Ashfords, years ago, developed this town, but it was like his great-great-grandpa or something. Or great-great-great. How many greats did I say?" I asked, blinking as the girls laughed.

At the sound of our laughter, Callum looked over at us, and I froze like a deer in headlights. Bambi, scared in the meadow and unsure of what to do with wobbly legs. But then he lifted his chin, and I waved at him, smiling.

Maybe I wasn't Bambi. Maybe I was the skunk who could learn to flirt and wave. I just hoped I wasn't the little rabbit, who spoke too much and slipped over their own feet. No, that sounded more like me.

"You know him?" one of the Ls whispered. I couldn't tell which one was which. That was probably an issue that I would deal with later.

"Yes, I know everyone who grew up in Ashford Creek. We're a small town. And he's friends with Rune and Atlas."

"Oh," two of them said at the same time, their voices breathy.

I just shook my head and smiled as Callum walked over.

"Here he comes. How do I look?" Laurelin asked, sliding her hands down her tiny, red dress.

Jealousy bit at me, and I pushed away that irritation. No, I wasn't going to let that have any hold over me. After all, the girls wouldn't be back, most likely, and it wasn't like Callum was for me.

"Happy birthday, Felicity," he whisper-growled, and my knees nearly went weak.

"Thanks, Callum. Buy me a drink?" I asked, trying to act like an adult. Because I was one. Damn it. "Or I'll buy you one."

He looked down at my nearly full drink and winked. "I'll buy you a soda, little flower."

One of the girls sighed behind me, and I blushed. "How about another time then? It's my twenty-first birthday, after all? I'm legal."

Something went over Callum's eyes, but I couldn't tell what it was. Instead, he nodded. "Another time. Though you're in Denver now, right? Not up in Ashford Creek that often."

"You never know. I could come home. I love home."

He shook his head. "There's so much more out there than Ashford Creek, little flower. You should go out and see it." And with that, he lifted his chin at the other girls and made his way back to the bar and Rune.

"I have so many questions," Laura whispered, and I just grinned before draining the rest of my drink.

"Brother's best friend and all that," I said with a shrug.

"Well, he's not my brother's best friend, so maybe I have a chance," Laurel slurred.

"Didn't you just try to hit on my brother?" I asked with a bite.

"Maybe. But it's Ashford Creek. There's nobody else here. It's a small town on a mountaintop. With nothing."

"Hey, it's my small town."

"That's right," Laurelin said as she wrapped her arm around my shoulders. "Be nice."

"I'm mean when I drink, I'm sorry."

"Forgiven. But you owe me a drink."

"Like you're paying for a single drink tonight," Laura whispered, and the four of us laughed, walking back out on the dance floor.

We danced for another hour, and I tried to keep up with my water, but I was dizzy. By the time I was back at my brother's house, tucked into his guest room with all of my friends, I was nauseous, regretting that last drink, and ignoring the roll of Rune's eyes.

"You're lucky I love you and you're staying here. Mom and Dad might not have been too happy about you drinking as much as you did."

I smiled brightly, my head pounding only slightly. "I didn't mean to. They were free."

"We'll teach you how to take care of yourself better next time, okay?" He leaned forward and kissed my forehead before making his way out of the guest room. I blinked a couple of times, wondering if I saw another shadow beside him. But it was such a *wide* shadow. Was it Callum? No. It wouldn't be Callum. He was just the man of my dreams.

I let out a sad sigh, curling into my blankets. Rune had two double beds in his guest room, so the girls and I were sharing, with one of them on the floor on an air mattress.

We could have stayed at my parents' house, but Rune had known we would be out late, so we'd stayed here. My family was amazing.

And considering what I knew the Ashfords had gone through, I was grateful for the home I grew up in. Part of me wondered if I would come back. If this would be my home. I ignored that part as dizziness took over, and I scrambled to the bathroom.

It turned out that having my brother hold my hair as I emptied the contents of my stomach wasn't the greatest way to celebrate my twenty-first birth-day. Especially when I knew for a fact that it was Callum leaning against the doorway, holding my water glass.

"Happy birthday," I whispered to myself.

"We'll take care of you, little flower. Don't worry."

And while I believed him, I couldn't believe I was once again careless.

With my night, with what I had drank, and with my feelings for him.

CHAPTER 2

Callum

"Seriously, is there a reason we're at your house and not the Summit Grill?" Teagan asked as she leaned against my kitchen island.

I rolled my eyes at my younger sister but couldn't help the twitch of my lips. "Just because you have a crush on Rune doesn't mean we should be spending all our time at his place." Beer sprayed over the edge of the counter, and I glared. "Seriously? You're an adult. In your thirties. Clean up after yourself."

My sister snarled. "Fuck you, I'm thirty. And what the hell? I do not have a crush on Rune."

"Wait, who has a crush on Rune?" Finnian asked as he strolled into the kitchen, his twin Sterling at his side.

"Teagan," I said as if it were true. It wasn't, but I enjoyed fucking with my sister. If I could continue to keep the light on a fake crush when it came to my sister and my best friend, I could ignore the actual feelings going on deep inside me.

Very deep. So deep, I was going to suppress them slightly more so I wouldn't have to think about them again.

See? Perfection. I wasn't thinking about Rune's little sister's curvy body and the fact that she could fit against me perfectly. And the way that she giggled and pressed her finger to my chest, batting her eyelashes.

That was little Felicity Carter. Yes, she was twenty-one now. Yes, the last time I had really hung out with her at any point, we had both been children, but I was still too damn old for her.

I'd lived lifetimes since then, and I was an old bastard for even thinking about her that way.

It hadn't stopped me from fucking my soaked-up fist in the shower after I had come home from the bar that night, but that was my own problem. I was going to hell, but at least I could get myself off before I got there.

"Excuse me," Teagan said, snapping her fingers in front of me. "Listen to me."

"What?" I snapped. My lips still twitched, however, thinking of Rune and Teagan and the fact that there would be zero chance of anything happening between them.

"I do not have a crush on Rune. And if you tell him I do, and he tries to give me a wedgie again like we're kids, I'm going to kick your ass. You may be the Ashford Creek NFL legend, but I can still kick your ass."

My younger brothers just laughed, Finnian full-out body quaking, as Sterling just shook his head, his rough chuckle filling the kitchen.

Bodhi finally walked in at that moment, looked at the group of us, and sighed before going to the fridge and pulling out a beer. "Do I want to know?"

"Callum has something up his ass and is fucking with Teagan by saying she wants Rune," Sterling explained.

"What's new?" Bodhi growled before he leaned against the counter. He folded his arms over his chest and glared.

It was a nice glare compared to his normal death one, so I figured he was in a better mood than usual. The fact that he'd even shown up to family dinner was proof that maybe he wasn't such a badger afraid to leave is den.

Although maybe I was just like him.

No, I wasn't. I was worse. I was like the other one. The other man that I saw whenever I looked down at my hands. Because they weren't my hands. They were my father's hands.

And maybe that was enough beer for me. Even though it was damn good beer.

"I'm just fucking with you," I said after a moment, having ignored the way that my siblings—minus Bodhi—snapped at each other good-naturedly.

Teagan tilted her head as she studied my face as if trying to figure out why I kept fucking with her. I probably should be more careful since she always saw far too much. "I feel like I need to punch Rune in the stomach just in case."

I rolled my eyes. "Maybe. But I do know that you could take Rune."

"Damn straight." Teagan beamed. "And with the way that Briar is being all mama bear, our baby sister could probably take him too."

That made me grin as the others tried to decide who could kick Rune's ass. To be honest, none of us could. Well, maybe a few friends who were out of town and still playing in their professional sports. I was long since retired and couldn't take a beating like I used to.

Which was why it was probably a good thing that I was staying away from Felicity. Because Rune could kick my ass. He ran the bar and grill in town, the only place that stayed open until two o'clock these days. Every once in a while, another bar would open, but it wouldn't last long against Rune's clientele.

Because it wasn't as if he let any shadowy figures walk through the doors. No, he took care of his people, and that was why he was my best friend. But that also meant that Rune had to kick out anybody who fucked with him. Hence, the guy who probably had to walk sideways through the doorway.

"How is Briar? All she does is text me back. Somebody's too busy to answer an actual phone call," Finnian said as he grinned.

"Well, it's because you keep bothering her." Sterling stole a chip from the bowl in front of him, and I pushed it toward him.

"Everybody start helping with dinner. We're having fajitas, and I've sliced most of the veggies. Bodhi, you want to go check the grill?"

"On it." He looked over his shoulder before he walked out to the deck. "And I talked with Briar this morning. She, the husband, and the most precious baby girl out there are staying in Texas for a bit. We'll get her to family dinner soon."

I met Teagan's gaze, and she was the one who shook her head.

"No, we'll go down there. It would be easier than her coming up to Ashford Creek."

Bodhi nodded tightly, a knowing look on his face. Because Bodhi wouldn't be leaving town. He either came to my place or hid up in his cabin in the woods. There were good reasons for that, and frankly, I didn't blame him.

But Briar wouldn't be coming up to Ashford Creek anytime soon if she was staying and being super careful.

She was not only a Grammy Award-winning songwriter; she was married to one of the hottest rock stars on the planet at the moment. They were new parents, newlyweds, and out on a world tour. They didn't need to come back to a town full of shadows and secrets. Secrets I was going to fucking uncover if it was the last thing I did.

Though the rest of my family didn't need to know that.

However, as soon as Briar stepped foot into Ashford Creek, not only would the town jump on her, wanting to know more about her life, about why she had run away from town, but the one person that I continually tried to protect her from would show up.

And I'd be damned if that man ruined anything else in our lives.

"Are the kids with Promise?" Sterling asked, taking a sip of his beer.

Finnian nodded. "It's her night," he answered, speaking of his ex-girlfriend.

Finnian and Promise had been high school sweethearts and ended up with twin daughters. They weren't together anymore and were figuring out co-parenting better than I thought they could.

I wasn't sure how they had ended up being nearly best friends out of it all, but maybe when you loved somebody, that's what you did. You found out that maybe you didn't love somebody the right way, and you wanted to protect your kids.

Both Promise and Finnian were finishing their

college degrees, parenting the twins, and each living with family. Promise with her parents, and Finnian with me for now. There was no way that we'd ever let the twins near their grandfather. I suppressed a shudder at that.

No, the world would do better if Matthew Ashford never stepped foot in Ashford Creek or in this world again. But he was the town drunk for a reason. And he would find a way to embarrass us all at any moment now.

No wonder Briar never wanted to come back.

Finnian pulled out his phone and, instead of helping cook, showed off the latest pictures he'd taken of the girls.

I rolled my eyes and went back to chopping, knowing that I was damn lucky to have all of my kids under my roof.

I might be their eldest brother, but I pretty much raised the twins and Briar. It wasn't as if my father was doing it.

After Mom had died, leaving seven kids behind, Teagan had stepped in, taking over that mothering role even though she had been far too young. It had killed me trying to help out, knowing that Teagan was putting her own feelings and future aside to make sure that the youngest could survive. I had put all of my effort into not only helping the younger kids but getting that scholarship. And when I'd gotten into college on a full-ride and ended up in the NFL—albeit a late-round draft pick, I had made enough money to buy the house we stood in, start my own business, and ensure that the rest of the family never had to go into debt to pay for school and could get out of Matthew Ashford's home.

"You know, I think this is the best IPA you've made," Sterling said, and I nodded tightly.

"I'm just glad that you're old enough to drink it now," I said dryly.

"I prefer the Pilsner." Teagan shrugged. "I'm not an IPA person, sorry. I don't like to chew my beer."

"Please do not get her started on IPAs," Finnian said with a dramatic sigh. "Do you know what your yearly special is going to be yet?"

I did, but I wasn't about to tell them. They wouldn't mean to, but they would tell one person, and then they would tell another, and suddenly Ashford Brews would make not only the local paper but the next town over, and my secrets would be out.

We were a decent business for the town, and my two years in the NFL had made sure that I at least had an entryway into this random life of mine. Maybe if I hadn't gotten hurt, things would've been different, but I was home, making this work.

I might surround myself with shadows and secrets in Ashford Creek, but I knew I was running away from them too.

For a damn reason.

But it wasn't as if I was going to let my family deal with those problems. They dealt with enough as it was.

"Here, I'll finish up the guacamole," Teagan said as she rubbed her shoulder against my upper arm.

"I forgot how short you were," I said, trying to push the darkness from my mind.

She rolled her eyes. "I'm taller than Briar."

"Well, she's not here, is she?" Teagan's eyes filled, and I cursed. "What? What did I say?"

"Just thinking about who else isn't here." She looked across my open-concept kitchen into the dining room, and I sighed.

Malcolm. That's who wasn't here.

Bodhi's twin brother, the rock star of the family, literally. A drummer prodigy who had made us all so fucking proud. I still couldn't quite believe that it had been over three years now. Three years since Malcolm had died in a bus crash while he was on tour. A bus crash that had nearly taken Briar out along the way.

Briar had come back to Ashford Creek to heal and had ended up needing her future husband more than she needed us, and I understood that.

We Ashfords knew how to remind others of their own darkness.

"I love you, Teagan," I said as I wrapped my arm around her shoulders.

"Love you too, you oaf."

"Why am I an oaf?"

"Because I don't have a crush on Rune."

"The more you say it, the more I feel like it's real," Finnian teased.

"I'm going to throw this avocado seed at you."

"If you do, then you have to clean up the mess," Sterling said as he took the plate of lettuce and tomatoes from me. "Go sit. We'll handle this."

I sighed. "Okay, but don't you dare get out the yellow cheese. You know the rules. No yellow cheese when we make Tex-Mex in this house."

We grumbled about it, but I just laughed, taking a seat at the long table that I had pried out of Bodhi's hands when he had finished making it.

"I do like family dinners," Finnian said after a while. My belly was full, and I had another beer in my hand. I'd only had two, but I wasn't planning on anymore. I did not need to get drunk tonight, not when I knew one of Dad's old friends had spotted him in town. Somebody needed to be alert.

"You only like it because you didn't have to pay for it." Teagan shook her head, a smile playing on her face.

Finnian gave a mock gasp. "Hey, I'm a single father of two. I need to save money."

Teagan rolled her eyes and I sat back and watched the show. "You say that as if Promise isn't the best ex-girlfriend in the world who co-parents with you in an organized way to the point that it scares me."

My brother shrugged before digging into his food. "True, I love Promise, and I'm so glad she's my daughters' mother. But I'm also relieved that we figured out this whole co-parenting thing after a rough patch."

"Is she going to open that bed and breakfast when she gets through college?" Teagan asked.

Finnian nodded. "That's the plan. There used to be one up Heritage Street, and I know she's is+ looking at the deeds now along with her family's help."

"That would be a great place for it. And you'd

help her fix it up, right?" Teagan asked as she played with the rest of her food.

There was something going on in my little sister's head, and I would figure it out. I would figure it out with all of them. I just hated the fact that I couldn't fix everything for them.

"That's the plan. Once I finish this program, I have to go through an apprenticeship. But I'm going to end up with all of my certifications. The town needs my special hands," he said as he wiggled his fingers.

"More like spirit fingers," Sterling teased under his breath, and I growled as Finnian lifted a chip to throw it across the table.

"We are not children, no food fights in my fucking house."

"Yes, Daddy," Finnian said with a roll of his eyes.

How the nicest and yet most sarcastic one of us ended up a father of two, I would never know. Because the man was one of the best fathers I'd ever seen. He didn't have a blueprint for it, though, considering our father, so I was just damn happy that Finnian was figuring it out.

"So, did you see who's back in town for the week?" Finnian asked again, and I tried not to look too alert. After all, my brother was talking to Sterling and Bodhi, not me.

"I cannot believe that Felicity's already twenty-one. Wasn't she just in braces?"

"You say that as if you aren't only eighteen months or so older than her," Teagan said dryly.

"And those eighteen months count. We've seen worlds since then." Finnian rolled his shoulders back, looking like the pompous jackass he sometimes pretended to be.

"She's almost done with college. What do you think she's going to do after that?" Teagan asked.

Finnian took a big bite of his food and thankfully swallowed before answering. "No clue. Though with Rune here, and her parents, she might want to come back."

"Why would she come back to Ashford Creek?" I asked, my voice low. "There's nothing for her here."

Bodhi gave me a look that I couldn't read, or rather, I didn't want to read, so I ignored him.

"There's plenty in Ashford Creek and we're growing yearly," Sterling said with a shrug.

"We might not be the center family anymore, with the town mayor in our pocket or growing the town's population and lines, but the town itself is cleaning up and getting a good reputation. Your brewery's helping with that. With the addition of the bar and grill room put in, and maybe this bed and breakfast, we're kicking ass." Teagan shrugged as if she hadn't tried to cement our family into this town once again.

"Not to mention your gift shop," Finnian said with a grin.

"It's not my gift shop. I only manage it," Teagan said as she continued not to eat her food. What the hell was going on with her?

"I'm thinking about maybe coming back to town after I finish culinary school," Sterling blurted.

I blinked and set my fork down. "What? Why?"

"The town could use a higher-end restaurant. You know, for the tourists that don't want to stay in the resort town. Summit Grill is great, as are the diner and bakery..."

"The bakery's shit, and we all know it," Bodhi grumbled but didn't elaborate.

Nobody needed to. Not with the owner and the way she constantly annoyed the fuck out of everybody in town. And frankly, her baked goods didn't rise to the occasion. I could not believe I just said that own pun in my head, and I was grateful I hadn't said it aloud. Finnian would never let me live it down.

I leaned forward, focusing on my brother's words. "Restaurants are hard to maintain. It's not just knowing how to cook."

Sterling nodded, and I was grateful that he had taken my words at face value and not heard any underlining rudeness. Because I believed in all of my siblings. The fact that any of us had lofty dreams to begin with surprised me, considering how we had grown up.

"I have plans. I promise. I'm not going to throw all of my savings into a restaurant and bail right out the gate. I'm going to learn along the way and then come back to town after school and get it done. The town needs it."

"Well, I run more than two businesses at this point, so I don't mind helping with whatever you need," Teagan said with a grin.

I nodded. "You run part of my brewery, Bodhi's business, and you pretty much do everything for the fucking gift shop, even though the owners treat you like shit. And I know that you help Rune out sometimes."

"While you're crushing on him," Finnian teased and ducked when Teagan threw her chip.

"Seriously?" I snapped.

Teagan glared at each of us. "I'll clean it up."

Wincing, I squeezed her shoulder. "No, I'll clean it up. I started the Rune thing. I'm sorry."

Teagan raised a brow, and I probably shouldn't have offered to help clean that up. Because that meant she would wonder why I had pushed the whole Rune thing.

I was going to hell.

Again.

"Either way, if you come up with a business plan, we'll look at it."

I still had a shit ton of money because I had friends who knew how to invest, and I wanted my siblings to succeed. Even if I knew they wouldn't take my money at face value. No, they'd fight to pay me back. And that's why I was so damn glad I had raised my kids better than my dad had tried to raise us all.

By the time we were finished cleaning up, my phone buzzed, and I looked down at the readout.

Rune: Can you go and check Felicity? She had a hangover all day, despite how much water she had. I need to head to Summit Grill, and I don't like the fact that she's alone.

My dick perked up at the idea of seeing Felicity, and I needed to tone it down.

What the hell was wrong with me? I was over a

decade older than her. I was a lecher. A crude old man.

Not really. But enough.

Me: Sure. Anything for the kiddo.

Rune: I can't believe she's twenty-one now. She's an old lady.

Me: Don't let her hear you calling her old.

Rune: Truth.

"Everything okay?" Teagan asked, a frown on her face. "We were going to make dessert and play video games until we decide that we've kicked your ass long enough."

I rolled my eyes. "I need to check something out for Rune real quick, but I'll be right back."

"Leave a love letter from Teagan!" Finnian called out, and I threw my head back and laughed as Teagan ran out of the room and jumped on Finnian's back. They wrestled to the ground, and Sterling threw his elbows in, protecting his twin and his sister at the same time.

My family was full of menaces.

"What's really going on?" Bodhi asked, his voice low.

I swallowed hard, not wanting to worry my brother for no reason. "Felicity was hungover from her birthday, and Rune wants me to make sure that she's doing fine. He doesn't like leaving her alone, and her parents are out of town."

"She's staying with Rune, then? Interesting." Bodhi took another sip of an Ashford brew, and I shook my head.

"Rune's my best friend."

"Yes. He is."

And with that subtle remark, Bodhi turned on his heel and went to end the play-fight in the living room.

I grabbed my keys and phone and told myself that I was doing this because my best friend needed help.

Not that I wanted to make sure that Felicity was okay.

I was a damn idiot.

By the time I got to Rune's house, I told myself I would be five minutes and then go home. There was no reason to stay.

I needed to stop thinking about Felicity as a woman. She just needed to be a blob. A blur, if you will. Because my dick got hard whenever I thought of her, and that was fucking ridiculous.

I knocked on the door, confusing myself since I usually just walked right in. But now Felicity was here, and that felt wrong somehow.

She opened the door quickly, her eyes bright. She didn't look like she had a hangover. No, she didn't look sick at all.

Instead, she looked like my worst nightmare.

Tiny shorts that barely covered her ass, and I was pretty sure I could nearly see her pussy. An even tinier T-shirt that showed every inch of her boobs, as well as her hard nipples since she wasn't wearing a bra, and pink toenail polish.

That's all she wore.

Dear God, this was my test. This was my battle-field. My testament.

And I was going to fail it all.

"Callum! I didn't know you were coming over. I was just getting in the shower, and I'm grateful that I heard you knock on the door before I did."

Felicity. In the shower. Soapy.

There was no way I was going to be able to hide my hard-on for much longer.

I cleared my throat. "Rune wanted me to check on you. Make sure you weren't hungover."

Felicity rolled her eyes. "I'm fine. The four Ls left, and I think he wants to just make sure that the house didn't get completely destroyed when he was gone. But you can tell Mr. All-High-and-Mighty that I cleaned up after them, and the house is spotless.

I'm going to shower, make some soup, and go to bed early. Yes, I had a headache this morning, but I'm fine. He kept me properly hydrated. And oh, you're still standing on the porch. You should come in."

There was no way in hell I was going inside if she was going to shower. *No way in hell.*

"No, it's fine. I was just checking since he asked. I got to go back to the house. The family's there."

"You drove all the way out here on family dinner night just to check on me?" The confusion etched on her face would've been cute if I wasn't so careless with everything that I did these days.

"Rune asked. He's my best friend." If I kept repeating that, it would help me remember. Why were her shorts so tiny?

She blinked at me and smiled. "Yeah, he is. Well, I'm going to bed early, and the four Ls are at the hotel now. They wanted a bit of mountain city life before they headed back to school. But we have dinner plans tomorrow if you want to come by and visit."

"I have work. Lock the door behind me. And don't open doors for random men anymore." The growl in my voice bit, and when Felicity's face paled, I could have kicked myself. But if I made her not like me, it would make this whole thing easier. Instead, I turned on my heels and went back to my truck, grateful when I saw her close the door behind me.

I was just like my father. Careless. Cruel. Careless with my feelings, careless with whatever the hell was going on with my dick and its reaction to Felicity.

And if I didn't rein it in, I was careless with my anger too.

I wasn't going to become my father.

And that meant I had to try harder to stay away from Felicity.

CHAPTER 3

Felicity

What had just happened? Seriously. What the hell had just happened?

Why had Callum Ashford been at my door after dinner just to check on me? He could have called. Could have texted. Could have done anything. Instead, he showed up.

I frowned, tapping my foot against the carpet. Maybe he had only done it because, once again, he needed to take care of Rune's baby sister. But I wasn't a baby. Though, with the way that Rune treated me, maybe everybody was always going to think that.

I pulled my hair out of its bun and made my way to the shower. I hadn't been lying. I was going to shower and then cuddle up into a blanket with a book. There wasn't much out there that could compete with how amazing that idea was.

My phone buzzed, and I looked down at it, a bright smile on my face.

I answered, the video call coming in brightly, and the background sounds a little obnoxious. My brother's smiling face, including a lovely black eye and a cut on his chin, filled the screen.

"Atlas! What the hell happened? Are you okay?"

In answer, my brother glared. "What the hell are you wearing? Are you out in public in that? Go put some clothes on."

"If you're really going to talk about what I'm wearing, let's talk about the girl that was sitting on your lap in that photo that just hit the internet. Huh? What was she wearing? And frankly, I'm glad she was wearing that. Because she's allowed to wear whatever the fuck she wants. She's an adult. At least, I hope to hell she was over eighteen. So if she's an adult, she could do whatever she wants, and you can't judge. I'm not going to judge her. So step off."

Atlas merely blinked at me. "The circular reasoning of that, in which how I'm suddenly a bad guy and creeper, confuses me. And I don't know who that girl was."

I rolled my eyes as he flipped me off. Yay for big brothers. "You have so many women on your lap that you don't even know who she was?"

"No. She just showed up at the restaurant we were at. It wasn't even a dive bar or anything. She showed up and ended up on my lap. I tried to shove her off and then realized shoving off somebody so they hit the floor was probably not the best idea, so I put my hand around her waist to help her stand up. She giggled, said it was for a dare, then kissed my cheek. That was it."

"Oh, brother of mine. What are we going to do with you?"

"She didn't find out, did she?" he asked, his voice low.

I winced, knowing show *she* was. It seemed that whenever anybody tried to leave Ashford Creek, you couldn't truly do so. The past was always there to bite you in the ass. Or at least haunt you when you weren't expecting it.

"Probably. She does have a phone with social media on it. And knowing the town busybody baker, it's probably going to be in the town bulletin."

"Fuck. I'm not an asshole."

"I know you aren't. You're my favorite big brother who happens to play hockey."

"I'm your only big brother who happens to play hockey. And seriously, what are you wearing?"

"I'm wearing random clothes that I left here last time I was staying at Rune's because I was just cleaning up after the four Ls."

Atlas cringed. "Are they still there?"

"You don't need to keep the disgust in your voice when you talk about my friends from college."

"I do when they treat you like shit."

"They don't," I argued for what felt like the twentieth time.

"They use you."

"What could they possibly use me for? It's not like they're using me to get to you or Rune. You guys wouldn't touch my friends like that." Atlas's jaw tightened, and I gasped. "Which one?"

"None of them. But each of them has come onto me. It was awkward as hell. And I didn't like it. Despite what the press says, I don't like it when women constantly fawn over me. I'm not a lecher."

"I'm going to write that on your tombstone," I

grumbled. Of course, the four Ls had hit on Atlas. They were doing so with Rune and Callum the night before. I hadn't missed it when Laurel had sidled up to Rune and rubbed her body all over him. Then Laura had tried to do the same to Callum. It had taken all within me not to pull them by their hair and scream about how Ashford Creek was mine.

I wasn't too territorial about my brother because, hello, he was an adult who could do what he wanted with his dick. And frankly, I shouldn't be territorial at all when it came to Callum.

He wasn't mine.

"Did they really hit on you?"

"It doesn't matter. They're your friends, and I'll be better about them. I'm sorry that I'm an asshole. I'm just tired. We lost."

The dejection in his voice slapped me, and I cursed once again.

"I wasn't checking the scores. I was too busy cleaning up all the vomit, and well, I'm sorry, big brother. I'm sure you kicked ass."

He snorted, though the humor had long since fled his expression. "I let two in during the last period, so not too great. Coach wants to kick my ass."

"Are you in trouble?"

"No, maybe. We have a young D-line, and they're having issues, so I'm having to step up. It's just, well...it's work. I'm one of the old men on this team, and it takes me longer to recover." He pointed at his black eye. "This was from an elbow in the locker room."

I burst out laughing, even though I hated seeing Atlas hurt. "Are you serious?"

"Yes, because I'm an idiot. Or these young kids are idiots. I didn't realize how young they were. A couple are younger than you. Infants."

I scrunched up my nose. "I really would appreciate it if everybody would stop calling me young and infantile. I'm an adult. A woman. About to graduate college and get a full-time job. Maybe even get my own place."

"Why would you need your own place? You could live with Rune or Mom and Dad. Hell, live in my empty house that I have up there, and I only stay at when I'm in town."

I resisted the urge to roll my eyes because he was just never going to get it. That I was an adult. With fully functional feelings that sometimes needed space. It wasn't like I was going to go out and buy a place of my own and go into crippling debt without thinking about it, but it would be nice to think that maybe they would assume I wouldn't be alone. Or I would want to step out on my own.

But I didn't say any of that. It would just be talking to empty space at this point, when I knew everybody had their own words.

"Enough about me. Are you really okay? Did you put ice on that?"

"I did. Don't worry. I'm taking care of myself. I just wanted to see how you were after that lovely twenty-first birthday. How much of that puke was yours?"

"I made it into the toilet and only did so because of the sugar. But I'm fine because I drank water. That's what happens when you have a brother who owns a bar and grill, and his best friend owns a brewery. They make sure you're fully hydrated. I had to pee like one hundred times, but I digress."

"Too much information, little sister." He paused. "Wait. The four Ls made you clean up after them?"

"They were guests."

"So were you. And they're fucking adults too. I don't understand kids these days."

I truly didn't want to think of the four Ls at the moment. Not that we weren't friends, but because Atlas always got grumpy. "And on that note. I need to go shower. I feel gross, and I just want to go to bed."

His brows rose. "It's six thirty in the evening. I guess when you said you were an old lady, you meant it."

I rolled my eyes. "Have fun. Don't end up on the front page of the gossip column when I'm not looking."

"You know I will. I can't help it." He let out a sigh.

Poor guy. "I love you."

"You too, kiddo."

I said my goodbyes and went to take a shower. I was a little tired from cleaning up after the girls. They had cleaned up most of the things on their own. But any vomit that had been in the bathroom had made them feel queasy. I hadn't minded cleaning up after a hard night. After all, a job was a job. I'd worked in offices and retail all during college, and the four Ls hadn't. My parents had a steady income and had been able to send me to a nice college, but I still needed to work for room and board.

I didn't mind that I was a different socioeconomic level than my friends. I only minded that they dared put their hands on Callum. No, I wasn't going to think about that. No, no, no, no.

I was just stepping into the shower when my phone buzzed again.

Thankfully, it wasn't a video call, so I answered.

"Hey, Lauren. Everything okay?"

"Everything's great!" she practically squealed, the sound of music blaring through speakers likely behind her.

"It sounds like you guys are having fun," I teased as I shook my head. I put my face under the spray, careful not to get my hair wet, as I quickly began to wash.

"What's up?" I asked, wondering why she was calling me tonight.

"Go get that little black dress on and come meet us."

"I told you that I'm staying in tonight."

"No, you aren't. I've got you a date."

I sputtered, practically drowning myself in the shower. I quickly turned it off, ignoring the soap underneath my arms. "What?" I snapped as I put the phone to my ear. "I have a date?"

"Yes. We're going on a cinco date. I don't know if that's a thing because I don't know how to say double date or triple date. That makes no sense. But there are five guys and only four of us. And while Laurel wouldn't mind taking two home with her, the other guy wasn't feeling it. However, we showed him photos of you, and he's super excited to meet you."

I groaned. "Are you serious right now? I can't believe you just set me up with a random stranger."

"It's a blind date. And all of his friends vouched for him." Friends that they had literally just met. "And everyone seems like nice guys. Don't worry, we're all going to be together and have dinner. You don't even have to drink since I know you're going to have to drive home tonight. Just have fun. You deserve to have fun. This is your whole birthday weekend. We have to go back to school and finals and all that horrible stuff later. But Bradley's here now."

Bradley. Well, I wasn't going to let his name give me pause. Just because he had a douchey name, according to my brothers, didn't mean he was going to be a douche. After all, between my brothers and the Ashfords, we had ridiculous names. I was used to names that weren't exactly of the social club set.

"Where are we going, and what time do I need to be there?"

I listened as she explained everything, knowing I

was going with the punches and doing what they wanted yet again. However, maybe spending the night after my twenty-first birthday at my brother's home alone while reading a book wasn't exactly the way to spend it. I was in college. I was supposed to have fun. And I would.

I'd be sober tonight because I was driving, and I wasn't an idiot. And I'd go dancing. Or whatever this cinco date was.

I only had fifteen minutes to get ready, and thankfully, my hair was already done. I'd put it back up in a bun when I'd gotten in the shower, so now I let the long dark blonde strands fall down my back in somewhat curls. I plugged in the curling iron, set it to as high as it could go, and quickly redid my makeup. It took me eight minutes to do my makeup, lotion up, and reshave my legs, not because I was planning on getting some tonight. No thank you very much. But because I was going to wear that little black dress. Instead of the strappy high heels, I went with wedges because I didn't know exactly where we would end up, but I was going to have fun. The four Ls would all be there, so it wasn't like I was going to be alone with some guy. And I needed to get over whatever crush I had on Callum. He was never going to see me as anything but little Felicity. And I needed to get over him.

With two minutes to spare, I got into my car and headed out to the park near the resort less than an hour away. There was a little restaurant there that had music and dancing, and I was excited now. I had left a note for Rune, and I wasn't going to be a little old lady.

I turned up the music, sang along, and finally felt as if maybe this birthday weekend wasn't so fuddy-duddy, as Atlas would say.

I pulled into the parking lot and was grateful I'd found a spot since this place seemed to be the center of attention for the night.

"You're here!" Laurelin said as she threw up her hands. Then she practically jumped on top of me, and I was grateful that I could catch her without breaking an ankle.

"Hey there. Have you had any water?"

"I'm making sure she drinks water," a tall man with a deep voice said behind her. "I'm Chad."

"I'm Hansen," another man said.

They all introduced themselves, and I knew I was never going to be able to figure out who was who. Each of them had the exact same color hair, haircut, and country club set. One of them had a dimple in his chin, and the other had darker eyes, but frankly, they all looked as if they could just step off an influencer's photograph page and call it a day.

"Felicity, this is Bradley," Laura said as she fluttered her eyelashes.

"Bradley's about to go to law school, and he's a Pisces."

"Gemini, actually," Bradley said with a laugh. He looked at me then, his blue eyes bright, and blond hair that curled right at the edges since it looked like it was a little too long.

I swallowed hard and tried not to feel too awkward, though I knew it was most likely a lost cause. "It's nice to meet you too. I am sorry if you guys were waiting on me."

"No, we were just having fun. Let's go dancing." Laura winked at me and gave me a hug. "I'm sober. I'm making sure that the girls aren't having too much fun. But we're glad you're here. It's your birthday weekend."

"I'm glad I'm here too." I squeezed her hand and then let Bradley lead me to the dance floor.

The music buzzed through my system, as did the Red Bull that I drank. I was grateful that nobody was pushing alcohol on me because I just wanted to have fun tonight. Bradley was nice, a good dancer, and when I needed water, he led me to the station. I wasn't about to let him give me an open container. My parents and brothers had taught me better than that.

He leaned down, his breath warm on my neck, and I shifted away slightly, needing space. "So, what are you going to school for?"

"Business and accounting. Honestly, I'm really good with numbers, and I've been working with the town bookkeeper and accountant whenever I come to visit my hometown. I like it."

"That's all you want to do?"

I did not like his tone, but maybe some people didn't get it. Not everybody needed to be an astronaut or doctor or lawyer. "I like it. And some months will be harder than others, but it has weekends off. Meaning I can have a life outside of work."

"Well, that's a good ambition, then. I don't know if my dad ever found that balance with being a lawyer and all. But I enjoy school so far. I'm excited for law school in the fall."

"I almost looked into law school, but I think I like my path more for me. I don't think I have it in me."

"Not everybody does."

I gritted my teeth and told myself that he didn't mean that as a push at me. I was just oversensitive.

When the couples began to break from each other, taking walks near the small lake, Bradley lifted his chin and gestured towards the path.

"You want to take a walk? It's lit. You'll be safe."

I blinked at him, taking a look around to confirm what he'd said. "Okay. Since the others will be around too. I am a little warm."

"Then don't worry, I've got you, Felicity."

We walked down the path some more, and when he took my hand, I didn't pull away. After a couple of those false steps and conversation, he asked genuine questions and seemed to like hearing about Ashford Creek. I didn't mention my brother's name since he had said he was a hockey fan, but when I mentioned the town, his eyes widened.

"Wait, I know that name. Isn't Callum Ashford from there? The tight end that only made it two years before some dumb ass broke his femur? That break was so bad it still makes the rounds when the talk about shit injuries."

I winced. "Yes, he's from there. A family friend, actually."

"No shit? He was amazing. Probably could have

made more than a few bucks if he stayed in. But bad break and all. Literally."

"He's doing good for himself now, though."

"Yeah. But whatever he does now probably pales in comparison to being an NFL star. Just imagine it."

I wasn't sure I wanted to. Or could. That part of Callum's life seemed so far off in the past, it didn't even seem like the same Callum I knew.

When we made our way to a bench underneath a large tree, he gestured towards it. "Want to take a seat? Get to know one another?"

My hair stood on the back of my neck, and I shook my head. "Maybe we should be getting back. We're a little far."

"Oh, Felicity. Just take a seat. You'll be safe."

He kept saying that, but I felt anything but safe.

So when he tugged on my wrist, I pulled back. "No. I want to go back."

"Just a small town girl, after all? What the fuck, Felicity? You're walking out with me all alone and aren't going to let me touch you? Stupid bitch."

And then he pushed towards me, gripping the end of my skirt. I punched out, my fist connecting with his nose.

"Bitch!"

I turned to run, and he tugged on my hair. When

he pulled me back to him, I stomped on his inset with my shoes, and he grunted before I elbowed him in the gut. Between my brothers and *Miss Congeniality*, I'd learned a few things. And yet, as my pulse raced and bile filled my throat, it didn't feel like enough.

I ran then, my heels digging into the dirt. And then I left them behind, knowing I could run faster barefoot.

"Felicity!" he screamed.

But I kept going, except I had no idea where I was. This path didn't look familiar, and I couldn't see the others. Pulse racing, I ran off the path, through a copse of trees, and sat behind a bush, pulling out my phone.

I couldn't think, couldn't breathe, I could barely press my thumb against the screen, trying to dial.

And as soon as he answered, I let out a choking sob.

"Callum. I need you."

CHAPTER 4

Callum

"*Callum. I need you.*"

Her words kept echoing in my head as I gripped the steering wheel and sped down the back roads. If a cop tried to pull me over right now, he'd have to chase me to the lake. There was no way I was going to stop on my way to Felicity's side.

"Just stay where you are. I'm going to find you."

"I don't hear him anymore," she whispered, her voice soft.

She'd sounded strong yet terrified when she'd first called, but now her voice kept getting quieter, and I wasn't sure it was from wanting to hide from that man. No, it sounded worse.

"Just stay where you are," I repeated, my pulse racing. "I'm almost there."

"I know you are. I'm okay. I'm okay."

"Yes, you are, little flower. I'm almost there."

"I should tell my friends where I am."

"You can text them, but don't get off the line. I want to hear your voice, Felicity. Got me?"

"Okay. I trust you."

It was like a kick in the heart, and I swallowed hard. "I'm almost there."

My tires squealed as I turned into the parking lot, and I jumped out of the car just as I turned off the engine.

"Callum?"

I looked up to see one of the Ls. I had no idea which one it was and stomped towards them. "Where the fuck is Felicity?" I growled, even though I knew she could hear me on the other line.

The girl's eyes widened. "She was out with a guy. Bradley. On a date. Why are you here? Jealous much?"

I glared at her and one of the other girls, who seemed to be worse for wear. "Where. Is. She?"

She lifted her chin. "I'm not going to let her get hurt. If you go and chase her, I'll—"

"You fucking let her get hurt by going out alone with that asshole. He's lucky I haven't found him yet."

The girl's eyes widened as the other girl wobbled near her. "Oh my God. She was out by the lake. That way. I didn't know. I swear I didn't know."

"We'll talk about this later." I turned and ran down the path, keeping my phone to my ear as I heard Felicity's soft breath against the receiver. "Do you hear anything?"

"No. I should just get up and come to you. I'm sure he's not out there anymore."

My stomach clenched, thinking about what could happen. "No, I'll be right there."

I ran down the path, searching for the group of trees that she said she'd hidden in, but it was dark and everything looked the same. Fuck. I was going to have to have her make a noise, but I had no idea where this douchebag was.

"Callum, is that you?"

I paused where I was, searching, but I couldn't find her.

"There you are!" a voice growled on the line, and I ran. Full speed.

I didn't know what the hell I would come upon, but I knew if that kid touched her, I'd end him. I wouldn't care that it would be my father's hands once again beating someone to near death. I'd do it.

Nobody touched Felicity.

Felicity screamed, and there was a sound of skin against skin as somebody slapped another person, and I had to hope she was fighting.

I couldn't think about anything else.

I turned the corner and finally caught sight of the two of them. Felicity kicked out and ran as the guy chased after her. I moved quickly, heart thudding.

The moonlight danced over her skin as she ran barefoot. Her face was pale.

"Whore!" the kid called behind her.

She ran past me, skidding to a stop, but I kept moving toward the kid who only had a few moments left to breathe. I'd kill him.

"Fucking bitch," the kid snarled before glaring at me. "She's a tease. Calling her daddy out to save her? What the fuck. She was asking for it, man."

My fist connected with the kid's nose, the crunching sound satisfying. Of course, it looked as if Felicity had already broken it before I got to it, and when the kid wailed, I didn't care. I just hit him again.

"You little bastard. You put your hands on her. You're lucky I don't kill you." Another fist to the jaw. The kid tried to kick back, but I pinned him to the ground.

"My father's going to end you." Funny thing to say through the blood pouring from his mouth.

I snarled, leaning over him. "Your father can try, but if I bury your body right now, nobody's going to miss you."

Finally, alarm hit his eyes, and I spread my hand around the kid's throat. For a moment, it looked like my father's hands on my throat, a flash of memory, the feel of strength around my neck as I tried to gasp for breath. That burning in my lungs when I nearly passed out.

But no, this wasn't then. No, this was a little boy who had wanted to have something he couldn't. To forcibly take it.

"Do you want me to end you?"

"No, no," he rasped.

A hand on my shoulder, and I froze.

"I'm okay, don't kill him."

I swallowed hard, trying to find some semblance of control. "You like this kid enough for him to live?"

She squeezed my shoulder again. "I don't want you to get in trouble. He's worthless. I'm fine."

I caught a quick glance at her face, the paleness there, the sight of blood on her lip. Then, looked down at her feet—torn up and bloody from running in the forest barefoot. I turned back to the little creep. "You come at her again, you touch her again, you even think about her again, I'll kill you."

And that wasn't an empty threat. I'd do it.

"You're insane. Both of you are insane. It was just a little ass. What the hell's wrong with you?"

I squeezed a little harder around his neck, and the kid finally seemed to get it.

"Callum."

The fear in her voice was mixed with worry, and I finally let out a breath. I released my hold and stood up, not bothering to be careful where I kicked.

"What the hell?" a few voices said behind us, and I turned to see an entire group of people moving.

I pulled Felicity into my arms and ran my hands up and down her skin. "What hurts?"

"I'm fine," she whispered, but her teeth chattered.

I cursed again and just held her close.

"Felicity!" one of the Ls said, probably Laura or Lauren. I didn't fucking care.

"I'm fine," Felicity whispered against my chest as I just crushed her to me.

"What the hell did you do to him?" another kid asked, his polo askew.

"He attacked me," Felicity said as she pulled away from me slightly. But I wasn't about to let her go. "And he wouldn't take no for an answer."

The guys looked at her for a moment, and I was worried that they were going to stand up for their friend, but instead, two of them just sighed, and another lowered his head while the fourth came forward. My hand fisted at my side, and I glared at him.

The other kid held up both of his hands and shook his head. "I don't want any trouble. But we'll take him from here."

"Oh? You're just going to take him away, and we're not going to press charges? I don't fucking think so," one of the Ls said, chin raised. She surprised me, and from the way Felicity stiffened, it surprised her as well. Why the hell was she even hanging out with these girls?

"Stupid bitch," the boy growled beneath us, and

I looked down at him, narrowing my gaze. He shut up.

Felicity tugged on my shirt, once again bringing my attention to her. "I don't want to press charges. I just want to go home. Please, can I just go home?"

"What if *I* want to press charges?" the little weasel snarled.

"Shut up," the other kid said. "We'll take care of this. He's not going to be a problem." He turned to Felicity, gaze narrowed. "If you want to press charges, we'll vouch for you. He's a little dick weasel."

"Then why the hell did you want him to go on a date with her?" one of the girls asked, and thankfully, she looked sober.

The other kid's cheeks pinked. "His dad works with my dad. I knew he was an idiot, but I didn't realize the rumors were true, and he was actually a creep too."

"Are you kidding me?" Felicity asked as she slid her hand into mine, taking a step away from me. I didn't let go, but I knew I probably should. "That's why you thought it'd be okay for him to take me out alone? What the hell is wrong with you?" She looked between all of them, shaking her head. "What's wrong with all of you?" Her knees nearly buckled, and I wrapped my arm around her waist.

"Take care of him." I lifted my chin at the piece of shit struggling to stand. "I'm taking Felicity home." I stared at the sober girl. "You good to drive?"

She nodded, eyes wide. "Yes. I'm good. Felicity?"

"I'm fine, Laura. I'm fine."

I didn't think that was quite the truth, but I wasn't about to let go of her. Everything moved quickly after that. The guys half-dragged, half-fireman carried the idiot away, and I lifted Felicity into my arms.

"Callum," she gasped as she wrapped her arms around my neck.

"You don't have any shoes on." I paused. "Where are they?"

"I kicked them off when I was running. I was wearing wedges, and it was harder to move with them on."

"Good girl." I struggled with my control once more. "The guy looked like he had a beating or two before I got to him." My jaw tensed, and it took all within me not to go back and kill the kid. That was the anger that ran through my veins. The carelessness. The Ashford.

And I wouldn't let Felicity see any more of it.

"My father and brothers taught me to defend myself. I didn't think I'd ever have to use it."

I cursed under my breath. "Let's get you home."

"Thank you for coming for me," she said, nestling her head underneath my neck.

"I'll always be there for you, Felicity. Always."

And as I got her into my truck, and headed back to Ashford Creek, I had to wonder to myself why exactly she had called me instead of her brothers, instead of anyone else. But I didn't want to think about that, nor did I didn't want to focus on the fact that I was damn glad she had.

***

The next morning, jaw tight after a sleepless night, I answered the door.

Felicity stood there, face clear of makeup, her hair flowing around her shoulders. She had on an old sweatshirt of one of her brothers and jeans with a hole in the knee. She wore tennis shoes and a cross-body bag, looking so different than she had the night before.

There was a slight bruise on her chin, and I

wanted to go back and find that little asshole to teach him another lesson he'd probably forget.

"Rune said you slept well. That's good," I said before she could speak.

I'd called her brother as soon as I dropped her off, and the man had run back home, letting his team take care of the bar. Rune had given me one questioning glance before focusing on his baby sister.

"Thank you for taking care of my sister," he'd whispered to me, and I nodded tightly, not knowing what to say. Because I was a fucking bastard when it came to Felicity Carter. And no one else needed to know that.

"I'm okay. The girls all called to apologize, and I will have to go back and talk to them since I still have a couple more weeks as their roommate, but I'm okay."

I wasn't about to touch that since I didn't understand why she hung out with them to begin with. "You're not going to press charges?"

She shook her head, hands in front of her. "I just don't want to think about it. Okay? Nothing happened."

I raised a brow but took a step back. "It's getting

colder out there. You shouldn't be standing on the porch."

And I shouldn't be letting her inside.

Her shoulders sagged in relief as she stepped forward.

I closed the door behind her and raised a brow. "You should be at home resting. Or going back to school."

"I will. I promise. I just wanted to say thank you. For being there. For dropping everything and coming to me. I don't know why I called you first... I just knew you would be there."

She shrugged as if it meant nothing, and I couldn't let it mean anything. Because if I let her call me again, to reach out, it would be too much. She would see too much. I needed to nip this in the bud right then and there.

"Don't think of me as a white knight," I snapped, and her eyes widened.

"Callum."

"No. I'll break you just like I nearly broke him. You get that, don't you? Don't be careless with your life. Because I'm not always going to be there to save you." I knew the words were cruel, but I needed to push her away. Needed to get that look out of her eyes. Because I recognized that look. It was the same look I wanted to feel. And damn that. Damn whatever the hell mounted between us.

"I don't need you to save me."

I raised a brow. "You called me. And yes, you do need me to save you, little flower. You're a kid. You're fucking Bambi." Cruel words, and yet she didn't back down.

Instead, she did the worst thing possible. She stepped forward, put her hand on my chest, went to her tiptoes, and pressed her lips to mine.

I cursed and knew I should push her away.

But I didn't.

Instead, I broke.

I wrapped my hand around the side of her neck, my thumb below her chin, my fingers digging into her flesh, as I crushed my mouth to hers, kissing her harder. She moaned, a little gasp of surprise, as my tongue flicked along hers. The kiss went on and on, exploring, deepening, and it took all within me not to lift her up by those hips of hers, press her against the back of the door, pull down those jeans, and slide my cock right into that tight pussy.

But she was already bruised, already hurting, and already scared.

And I wasn't that man.

Abruptly, I pulled away and pushed at her side slightly.

She staggered back, and I nearly reached out for her. Regret shamed me, but I didn't touch her again. Instead, I stood there, chest heaving, as she stared up at me, looking like fucking sweet with her eyes wide and her lips swollen.

"I'm not a good man, Felicity. Just stay away. It'll be good for both of us."

And then I stomped out the back door, leaving her alone in my house, and knowing that the taste of her would be forever branded into my lips.

I was a careless man, and I did not deserve Felicity Carter.

And that would be the last time I let myself break.

Find the rest of Callum & Felicity's romance in Legacy !!

BEFORE I KNEW

BEFORE I KNEW

It all began with a wrong number.

When Blakely gets added to the Cage family group chat, chaos ensues. What she doesn't expect is to have a side chat with the eldest brother.

What was supposed to be a simple sign off, turns into a mild flirtation and invitation to lunch.

Only Aston Cage has his secrets.

And perhaps they should've left their conversation on read.

Before I Knew is the prequel to the Cage family series. Learn how Blakely and Aston met, before they finally get their happily ever after in The Forever Rule.

ME:

Wait. Why did we make a group chat? I thought we already had a group chat? One with a name and everything.

FLYNN:

We had to make a new one because somebody ruined the last one.

DORIAN:

I feel like there was a little sarcasm in your pointed tone.

HUDSON:

How do you hear tone in a text message?

THEO:

Oh, we read tone.

FORD:

Seriously though, why the new group chat? Do you understand how many group chats I have?

FLYNN:

It's not our fault that you decided to marry two people who had large families.

HUDSON:

Greer's is a large family with three brothers and a bunch of spouses. Noah's family? Calling the Montgomerys large is like saying the earth is part of the solar system.

DORIAN:

That wasn't even a good analogy. You should have said something like water is wet.

THEO:

Oh, so are we making fun of Hudson's bad analogy here? Because I'm here for it.

ME:

I still want to know why we have a new group chat. Why we're even starting with the group chat.

FLYNN:

Because Dorian added his ex to the previous group chat, and I didn't know how to quietly remove her without notifying her.

ME:

Are you serious? She was in there the whole time.

HUDSON:

You don't just add someone to the group chat. You make a separate group chat.

THEO:

That's the whole rule of group chats. What is said in group chat, stays in group chat.

HUDSON:

Until you take a screenshot of your chat and then you put it in the other chat hoping that the person that you're talking shit about doesn't actually see it. And now I've confused myself.

ME:

I hate all of you.

FORD:

You love us. Seriously though, do not add spouses to the family group chat. Or parents. We have a family group chat with the parents, and then a family group chat with just Mom, and then one with just Dad. Hence why I'm very confused why we continue to have more of them. We need to name this one.

ME:

Let's just call it the Cages.

FLYNN:

Yes, because we don't have anything called the Cages in the Cage family group chat. You're the CEO of this family, what the hell's wrong with you?

HUDSON:

He's the president of Cage Enterprises. Not the CEO of the family.

FLYNN:

For a man that doesn't work with the company, you do sound a little testy.

DORIAN:

Those sound like fighting words to me.

JAMES:

I have been in a meeting this entire time. Are we seriously just going to have a fifty-message long group chat about the efficacies and rules of group chat? This isn't Fight Club.

THEO:

All the more reason to actually speak about the group chat, as we're allowed to talk about it. Like you said, this isn't Fight Club.

FORD:

I thought we weren't supposed to talk about fight club.

HUDSON:

That movie came out what, fifty years ago at this point?

FLYNN:

Let's not let Hudson do math anymore.

ME:

Seriously. Now that we know we have a new group chat, we can come up with a name later.

FLYNN:

Fine by me. Did you start this discourse for a reason, eldest brother of ours?

ME:

I wanted to ensure we were all ready for family dinner on Friday. You know, our favorite thing to do.

HUDSON:

Groan.

DORIAN:

I'm busy.

JAMES:

New phone, who's this?

THEO:

Yes, because that totally works, James. Wait. Does it work? I need to know. For reasons.

FORD:

I will probably have dinner with the Montgomerys. In fact, I'll make sure I'll have dinner with the Montgomerys.

ME:

Dad won't be there. He's on a work trip.

THEO:

I'm in.

HUDSON:

Friday night at six again?

DORIAN:

I might not make it until six thirty.

JAMES:

I'll be there. We can hitch a ride together, Flynn.

FLYNN:

What if I have a date?

DORIAN:

You guys, I can't laugh so hard that I pee myself in public. Flynn. A date.

FLYNN:

Your urinary tract problems aren't
my problems.

FORD:

I might have a Montgomery dinner,
but I'm going to try to make it.

ME:

Dinner is at seven. Drinks begin at
six. I suppose it's my turn to host.
Unless we'd like to go to The Teal
Door?

THEO:

Do not ruin my restaurant with a
family dinner that will surely be loud
and rowdy.

JAMES:

We are elite businessmen. We are
not rowdy.

DORIAN:

I'd rather go to the restaurant.

THEO:

You are not allowed to date any
more of my waitresses. One quit
already.

ME:

Dorian, what the hell did you do?

DORIAN:

I didn't do anything. Laura said she
was moving to be near her mom
because she got sick. I may like
women, but I don't fuck with them.

HUDSON:

Sure, Dorian. Whatever you say.

DORIAN:

I'm offended.

THEO:

You really aren't.

JAMES:

You really, really aren't.

ME:

We'll pick the place soon. But Theo,
is it okay if we use your place
instead? I'd rather not have to deal
with a caterer. I could cook, but I
don't have time.

THEO:

Fine. However, just know I'm going
to charge you out the ass.

ME:

Charge the company.

DORIAN:

Wait, you're not even going to cook
for us, Aston?

ME:

I'm not in the mood to search for a middle finger emoji.

FLYNN:

My God, how old are you?

JAMES:

We don't ask those types of questions.

UNKNOWN NUMBER:

Hello? Do you know how to exit a group chat? Not that this hasn't been enlightening, but I don't think I'm supposed to be here.

I leaned back and stared at my phone as if it were a snake ready to strike. I did not recognize the number. It wasn't Dorian's ex. And now I was wondering why we had a complete stranger in our family group chat. Damn it. I picked up the phone as soon as it rang, Flynn's name appearing on the screen.

"Do you know who that is?" Flynn asked, his voice sounding slightly panicked.

"Is it weird that I hope it's someone that Dorian met and accidentally put her number in?" Because having it be a complete stranger would be worse. At least we hadn't shared company and family issues within the chat. So far.

"We don't know if it's a *her*."

That was true. We didn't know if it was a <u>her</u>. And here I was, acting as if it could be. Weird.

"Hell, no one else is texting, so they're probably waiting for me to handle it?" I ask, pinching the bridge of my nose.

"Sounds about right. But you are the big brother. It's what you're used to. Handle it."

"At least we didn't discuss company secrets."

"No, we just said our names often enough that now someone has our numbers. Hopefully it's not the press. Or a rival. Fuck."

I could practically see Flynn pace his office. We weren't working in the same building today. Flynn was off in the small town that we had purchased over two generations ago, while I was in our high-rise in the city of Denver. I liked running Cage Enterprises. Our grandfather, and later our father, had built it from the ground up, and while they had made some questionable business choices along the way, we had changed the game. We worked with gaining financing and worked with ethical and environmentally friendly building. Hence why we worked with Ford's family, the Montgomerys so often. We worked with real estate development, small business backers, and environmental research.

Meaning we had way too many NDAs to begin with, and people were constantly trying to reach us.

And now, we were adding random people to group chats.

Again, the group chat went completely silent, and I copied the person's number before starting a new chat.

ME:

Sorry about that. Wrong number I assume?

The three little dots flared for a moment, before they went away, and I had to hope that that was for the best.

UNKNOWN NUMBER:

I wouldn't know. You're the one now texting me outside the group chat. Where did you get my number?

I studied the number, then quickly went through my contacts, and cursed under my breath. It was one away from Dorian's. Meaning, when Flynn had made the group chat, he had somehow typed in Dorian's number. Which didn't make any sense to me because you could just go through the contact list. I quickly called up Flynn again.

"How did you make the group chat?"

"My phone was giving me problems, so I just typed in everyone's numbers. I have them all memorized."

I rolled my eyes. "Of course you do. But you added one more you shouldn't have."

Flynn cursed under his breath. "Apparently I was tired."

"Apparently I have to clean up your messes."

"It's a chat. We'll delete it. Breathe."

I rolled my eyes at the fact that it was Flynn telling me to calm down now. That was rich. "You were the one panicking before. Because now this person has our numbers, our names, and where we'll be on Friday."

"Yes. Because she could be a sniper. We've just alerted our own demise where we'll be. It'll make it easy for them. But hopefully I'll have wine beforehand."

"I hate when you get all quick-witted after you're done panicking because you know I'll handle it."

"It's like you know me. Got to go. Meeting's starting."

I sighed, then gestured for James to come in as he walked across my office and set down a stack of papers. He raised a brow, and I sighed, gesturing toward the phone.

"I'll handle it."

"It's not anything to handle. But I'll see you soon."

"Yeah. You will."

I liked the fact that James and Flynn worked with me. I didn't feel like I was constantly searching to find my large family. I had way too many brothers to count. Okay, I had six brothers. With Flynn and Hudson as twins, Ford was the youngest, and I was the oldest. And yet Ford was the one who was married and happy and settling in his life. The rest of us were figuring out what we wanted. That was fine though, it wasn't as if my end of days were here. But I was busy with work, far too busy to deal with something like a relationship. Flynn and James worked hours just as long as I did.

And I knew Theo as a chef and a restaurant owner worked off hours, to the point that we rarely got to see him. Dorian was on the same hours as Theo since he owned a bar and grill that went for high class clientele even though the place was called The Cage of all things. I rolled my eyes at that.

Hudson and Ford were the only two that really didn't work for the company anymore. With Ford working for a security company that he owned with his spouse and his spouse's family, and Hudson painting for a living. It was odd to think that there was even an artist in our family, since it wasn't something that our father had really subscribed to. But Hudson had always gone his own way. After all, he had done his stint in the Army, spending far too many years overseas where we couldn't get ahold of him.

But now we were all here, doing something as casual as family dinner.

And apparently had just invited this stranger.

ME:

We're sorry for bothering you. You can just remove yourself from the group chat by hitting the information button.

UNKNOWN NUMBER:

Hmph. I should have thought of that. Sorry it's been a long day. But you guys sound hilarious. Brothers I take it?

I frowned, wondering why this person wanted the information, and why I wanted to answer.

ME:

Yes. Should I ask your name since you know mine?

UNKNOWN NUMBER:

You say that as if I could figure out who was who from the texts. There were a lot of them.

My lips curled into a smile.

ME:

Hazard a guess.

UNKNOWN:

I'm afraid to. But I assume you're the eldest from the way you're trying to take care of everything and texted me outside of the chat.

I frowned, wondering how this person could know this.

That was a little too intuitive and it made me uncomfortable.

ME:

And what's your name?

ME:

It seems only fair to ask.

UNKNOWN NUMBER:

Well, since you haven't asked for my location yet, I guess I can't be too worried about you being a serial killer.

ME:

I feel like I should be the one worried.

UNKNOWN NUMBER:

Blakely. My name's Blakely.

ME:

Well, Blakely. It is nice to meet you.

BLAKELY:

Nice to meet you as well. Although this isn't how I usually talk to men on phones or even on the internet. I don't like things like that. In fact, I should probably put my phone down before I realize you're a scam.

My lips twitch, and I did the one thing I should have done this whole time, I Googled the number.

And because the internet always showed everyone's secrets unless you knew how to hide them, I found it far too easily.

Blakely Graves.

I didn't look beyond the first page, but I wanted to make sure that she wasn't a scammer or anything. But Blakely Graves was a real person. And the photo attached to her profile that came from a job search site made my breath catch.

Gorgeous light eyes, blonde waves falling past her shoulders. And hell. Now I felt like the stalker here. Maybe I was the one asking for too much.

ME:

Anyway, I have to get back to work. But sorry for interrupting your day.

BLAKELY:

I've had a long and tedious day. So thanks for making me laugh. And you should totally cook for them. Not just do catering. At least one time.

I rolled my eyes.

ME:

Did you see how many of them there are? No thanks. Plus I don't want to poison them.

BLAKELY:

Good to know. Have a good day and I'll remove myself.

I looked at the chat and saw the notification that she had indeed removed herself from the chat. I didn't know why I felt a little sad about it. But I ignored it, and ignored the rest of the group chat as the brothers continued to talk now that they felt a bit safer after she left. Instead, I went back to work, my gaze looking at my phone every once in a while.

I didn't want her to text back. I didn't even know this person. I was just a little too tired.

I had been working too many long hours and knew the chaos was because I was trying to clean up a few messes my father had set to the side when he'd decided to retire. He was good at that. Making big promises and working on a few of them so they shone, and then letting everything else fall by the wayside. And I cleaned them up. Along with Flynn and the others, but it was mostly me.

And it wasn't as if Mom wanted anything to do with the company, or anything that came along with owning the town.

Because the Cages didn't just work in downtowns and across the world in high rises. No, we owned a whole town.

One in the mountains of Colorado, that was just for the Cages.

I had always thought as a child it was fun to have a town named after us, the one that held our legacy.

I just hadn't realized how much paperwork came with such an accolade.

Because we were not small town people. At least I didn't think so. My brothers on the other hand, they fit in a little bit more. Me though? I needed my suit and tie and martini. I wanted my Mercedes, and not the off-roader. I didn't want to deal with snow where we also had to be the ones who plowed.

I had too many other things on my mind.

Didn't that make me sound like a pompous ass.

I picked up my phone again, knowing I was distracted.

ME:

So do you think it's going to snow tomorrow?

I set down the phone again, wondering why I was even asking. It was ridiculous. But I couldn't get those eyes out of my head.

BLAKELY:

Probably. And then it'll be eighty degrees by the end of the day. It's Colorado. It's how we do weather.

ME:

So are you from here then?

I paused, wondering how to word it.

ME:

You have a Colorado number, so I just assumed you were local. But that doesn't mean anything anymore because we all have cell phones all over the world.

BLAKELY:

As soon as I typed my response, I realized the same thing. I don't even know why I replied.

BLAKELY:

But no, I'm from here. Born and bred. I wouldn't know where west is if I left. I need the mountains.

As the Rocky Mountains in Denver were always on the west, you always knew where north was. It did help with directions.

ME:

I got lost when I was in Central Pennsylvania once. We were in a valley, and I couldn't figure out where north was. It didn't help that it was overcast, and I couldn't see the sun.

BLAKELY:

You know our phones have compasses on them. And GPS.

ME:

Yes, but I couldn't look down when
I was driving. And I couldn't figure
out the rental car. It was a thing.

Now I felt embarrassed, like an idiot for even saying anything. I ran a multi-million-dollar corporation and several businesses, and I couldn't figure out a rental car. Or at least that one day had been a nightmare. I never showed weakness. That's how people took advantage of you. But apparently it was easy to do so over a single chat where neither of you knew the other in real life.

BLAKELY:

No it's okay. I'm the same way. I
have to get into a meeting though,
okay? Talk to you later?

BLAKELY:

Or not. Since we're strangers.

I smiled then, typing right back.

ME:

Talk to you later.

But we didn't, at least not that night. The next morning I was working, dealing with a thousand meetings and papers on my desk, and when the snow began to fall in earnest, I smiled and picked up my phone.

ME:

Well, it is indeed snowing.

BLAKELY:

Good thing I dressed in layers. I wonder what the weather will be like later today.

A few hours later, my phone buzzed.

BLAKELY:

It is 75 degrees outside. I do not understand this weather.

A few days later, I picked up the phone again when it buzzed.

BLAKELY:

Did you see that score last night?

ME:

Only a few glimpses of it. I didn't see the last save.

BLAKELY:

The Avs are my team for a reason.

ME:

Well, brand loyalty helps. Although I used to be a Penguins fan as well.

BLAKELY:

I can't believe you just said that. I think I'm going to have to delete your number.

ME:

That would be a horrible reason for you to do that.

BLAKELY:

Okay true. But tell me you're at least a Broncos fan.

ME:

I can neither confirm nor deny. But I do like going to the games.

We had box seats for the Avs as well, but I only got to go to those when we had to bring in partners and clients. I rarely got to enjoy myself with things like going to games and having fun. Maybe I did need a weekend out in the town. Cage Lake had a little inn where you could rest and relax—though Flynn was the only one of us who had stayed there as of yet. The Cages owned the resort and many of the buildings in town, but we didn't tend to live there. We each had homes along the lake though, so I could just head there. Though I knew Flynn was renting his out right now.

Maybe I needed a break. Maybe I needed to go to a game.

The next day, I was the one who texted first.

ME:

Did you see that game?

BLAKELY:

No I missed it. Deadline.

I didn't know what she did for a living, nor was I sure she knew that I was Aston Cage. It wasn't that I was famous or anything, but in certain circles, people knew who our family was. That's why we were always careful about who we let in. Dorian may have played around, but he was still damn careful.

Hence why a group chat could change things.

ME:

It was a good game. I wish I could have gone.

BLAKELY:

Maybe someday.

The next day I texted again.

ME:

Let's meet for coffee.

I hadn't even realized I was typing it until the

bubble exclaimed it was sent and there was no going back.

I just wanted to know who this woman was. I could have Googled more. I could have asked someone to look into her. The information was at my fingertips. But I couldn't get past my curiosity about the woman who made me laugh with just a few text messages.

BLAKELY:

I'm still not sure you're not a serial killer.

I grinned, grateful she was at least a little cautious. I sure as hell wasn't right then.

ME:

Public place and all. I promise I won't take you to a secondary location.

I wasn't sure if that sounded creepy or like a come on, but when she gave me a laughing emoji, my shoulders relaxed.

BLAKELY:

I shouldn't.

ME:

We should do it anyway.

BLAKELY:

Okay, that sounds like a good argument.

I straightened in my chair, my hand tightening around my phone.

ME:

Okay then. Tomorrow? Just coffee. No murder.

BLAKELY:

Okay. I can do that. Not the murder thing. Although all I know about you is that you live in Colorado. You could be hours away.

ME:

Meet me at Taboo. Do you know that place? It's downtown.

I could see the chat bubble light up again before she answered.

BLAKELY:

I know the place. And I work downtown. Coincidence.

Yeah, coincidence. Or maybe *she* was a serial killer.

I had a date with a wrong number.

And I didn't want to be wrong about *this*.

"I'm definitely going to be murdered, right?" I asked as I paced my bedroom.

My best friend Isabella stared at her phone while perched on the edge of my bed, her legs crossed, and a small frown on her face.

When she didn't say anything, I cleared my throat and asked again. "Am I really going to get murdered if I do this?"

Isabella put down her phone and looked up at me, a small smile playing on her face now. I had known Isabella for years and she was one of my best friends. She was also one of the most beautiful people I knew. Her whole family was, if I were honest. She had three gorgeous sisters, and her brother was a man who apparently made people swoon when he walked into a room. I had always thought of him as Isabella's younger brother, so that hadn't been a thing in my eyes. But now as I stared at my friend, I had to wonder if I'd lost my mind about the decisions I'd made.

"No. Maybe. I hope not."

"Not helpful." We grinned at each other before she shook her head.

"Honestly, a group chat? So they just entered your number and suddenly you were part of their meeting? That sounds a little suspicious."

"I know, right? But it does happen. You've heard of it happening. There was that whole viral moment where a grandma texted the wrong person inviting him to Thanksgiving, and then it turned into this heartwarming thing."

"I remember that. It's just all that had happened with a group chat. You usually have to add contacts."

"Maybe he typed it in. Who knows. But I was in there, and all of the people sounded like they were joking around and they were a family who cared about each other. A real family with sarcasm as their love language."

"And so the real family is why you're going to go on this coffee date?"

I ran my hands down my dove-gray slacks, and immediately went to take them off, knowing I needed to wear something different. Maybe a skirt. Yes, a skirt would be good.

"Are you getting naked for me for a reason?" Isabella asked, and I flipped her off before putting my pants back on. "I was thinking about wearing a skirt, but then that seemed a little too forward."

"You mean one of your A-line pencil skirts? No, that wouldn't be too forward. And we're going to be late and hit every ounce of rush hour if you don't make a decision. You look gorgeous, Blakely. Live in it. Be in it."

I held back a smile since she sounded like the trainer in the classic *Miss Congeniality*. "Thank you for coming over. I know you're busy and you don't have time to deal with my insecurities and the fact that I'm going on a blind date with a man I'm randomly texting about the weather and Avalanche games."

"I still can't believe he said he was a Penguins fan." Isabella held up her hand. "It's okay. We all have a thing for Crosby."

I gave her a wry smile as I met her reflection in the mirror. "I'm sure there are other guys on the team you know."

My best friend shrugged. "Well, I don't really pay attention to them unless they are my team. It's not like I have time."

"You work more hours than I do."

"Maybe. But it's what I do. It's life. Now, you look wonderful, for work, and for a simple coffee. I like Taboo. They have great sandwiches, and I go in for a different type of coffee every time. They seem to fit my moods. It's a little creepy actually."

"I'm going to a creepy coffee place to go meet a serial killer," I blurted, and Isabella let out a deep breath, calming herself while I did the same. She knew I was on a downward spiral, and I needed to lift myself out of it if there was any way for me to make it through the day.

"You've been to Taboo. You like their coffee. You also like the look of the very hot tattoo artist next door."

I bit my lip and inhaled before letting out a long breath. "That is true. And there's a bookstore that I love nearby. In fact, I love that whole street. It's like a little oasis in the middle of downtown. This is fine. It's just coffee. It's a public space."

"Do you know his name?" she asked.

I froze, realizing that I didn't. That seemed like a little oversight and yet I knew it was for a reason.

Being strangers in a text chain was easier to lean into than knowing who this man was. However I was about to meet him. "I don't. I don't even know what he looks like. I'm just going to meet some guy holding a phone in a coffee shop. I could sit next to anyone. This is so unlike me."

"Just Google his phone number and figure out who it is." Isabella reached for my phone, and I snatched it back, feeling a little protective of it. When she raised her brows, I winced.

"I don't know if I want to know."

"What are you worried about? That he is married? Someone you know? A ninety-year-old man?"

I put my face in my hand and groaned. "This is ridiculous. I should just look up his number."

"You should have done it weeks ago."

However, I did what I should and typed the number into my search engine.

"Do you really have it memorized?" Isabelle asked and I tried to ignore the humor in her tone.

I didn't look at her face, my cheeks burning. "We've been talking. It's been nice. And I've been looking at the number instead of a name because I couldn't add him to my contacts."

Yet everything changed with a single page load

on my browser. I shouldn't have been surprised that the world was a little ironic. Because as soon as the page loaded, I stood in my room, mouth agape as Isabella sucked in a breath.

"Aston Cage?" I blurted, my voice going high-pitched. "Aston Cage. Of the Cage family? *Cage Enterprises*?"

"Your voice is getting a little high-pitched."

My hands gripped my phone so tightly, my knuckles went white. "It should be. Aston Cage. I know this man."

Isabella's eyes shot up to mine. "You've met him before?"

I shook my head. "No, my boss just hates him. Because a lot of times we go for the same developments, and they win."

"Because the Cages are a little savvier than your boss. You know that. That's why you work for your boss. You're always fixing everything he messes up."

I held up my hand. "I don't have time to worry too much about that. But look at him. *Look at him.*" I held up my phone to her and waved it around.

"What am I supposed to be looking at? He looks like a dude. With hair. That seems to be a little dark. Sometimes he has a beard in these photos, sometimes not. And he looks to do a lot of galas. That sounds boring."

I turned the phone back to me, and scrolled, realizing that he was indeed on the arm of a different woman in practically each one. Gorgeous statuesque women and variety of color of dresses. All for galas. "Oh, this is so stupid. This is Aston Cage. That means I was in the group chat of the *Cage family*."

"They aren't gods. Though your boss would've loved that."

My gaze shot to hers. "He can never find out. No wonder they all ghosted the chat right before I left. They had to be freaking out."

"It's not like they're going to divulge family and business secrets in a group chat. At least I would hope not. They seem smarter than that."

"But it's *Aston Cage*."

"Is he a playboy or something? I'm an accountant. I don't know these things," Isabella said with a sigh.

"You're a brilliant accountant, and no, I don't think so. Maybe. That doesn't matter. He's gorgeous."

"He's a man."

I laughed at that, shaking my head. "Maybe

you're the one who needs to go out and meet somebody."

"The next time I get added to a family group chat, maybe I will. But I have enough in my life to deal with. Especially because we're going to be late. Now go to this coffee thing. Let one of us live a little. You're going to be fine."

"I can't believe you of all people are the one pushing me into this."

"I'm living vicariously through you. Your job is more fun, your life is more fun, and you're going to meet a CEO who could take over the world. I don't see the problem here."

"I see a very big problem here."

"What's the worst that can happen?" she asked, sounding so much unlike Isabella, I was afraid we had somehow switched places.

"Are you kidding me right now?"

"I have your phone tracked, and I'll put an AirTag on you. I'll know where you are at all times."

"That sounds a little more like the real Isabella," I said with a laugh, as I hugged her tightly. She patted my back, and then pushed off me.

"Now let's go. I'm not in the mood to deal with assholes on the highway. Which is every day."

"Thank you for getting here before the sun even rose."

"It's because I love you. And I needed to make sure that our tracking is going well."

I laughed at her, and we made our way to our respective jobs, that tension writing the back of my mind the entire time.

Work seemed to go at a slog all day. I enjoyed my job. I enjoyed strengthening businesses and figuring out which player was best for which position, but my boss of Howard Enterprises didn't play well with my ideas. But it was my job to make sure that we didn't go under and break the rules.

I wasn't a CEO. I wasn't a CFO. I was someone who had to have my hands in a thousand pots at once. And I enjoyed it. That meant I had to keep my mind on task, and I wasn't doing it very well because I was sitting here wondering what the hell I was going to do.

"Blakely, do you have the report?" Mr. Howard said from my doorway, and I smiled at him. The man didn't specify which report and could have just emailed me. He didn't have to walk across the office just to ask me about a report that was probably already in his inbox and printed out in triplicate because that's how he liked things. Who needed to save trees?

"Which report?" I asked.

He scowled at me, and I knew that was probably the wrong thing to say. "You know, the report. The one I've been waiting on."

"It should be in your inbox." Again, I had no idea what report he was talking about, because *he* didn't know what report he was talking about, but I was up to date on what he needed from me, so it would be in his inbox. His team of assistants should have already handled it, but he liked to look grumpy and in charge on the floor. It lent a sense of control that I didn't understand, but he said it worked.

I had to remind myself I really loved my job when people did what they were supposed to do. Even though it wasn't my biggest fan right now.

"Good, good. You're still on for the gala this weekend?"

"I'll be there. It's a lovely charity event."

"Yes, but we have to make sure we don't let the Cages outshine us. You know them. They always like to walk around like little peacocks, pluming their little feathers."

I wasn't even sure that was true, but I did my

best to keep a straight face. Because I was about to go on a coffee date with the head peacock.

Oh, God. This was such a bad idea.

"I will do my best to not let them take over."

"Good. It's a charity event, and we need to make a stand."

It was a charity event and that meant we should probably give to charity and raise awareness, but sure, making a stand worked. With that, Mr. Howard stomped off, probably to go growl at someone else, and I looked down at my phone, and realized I had fifteen minutes to get to Taboo. I quickly set everything as idle, nodded at my assistant, and made my way down the high-rise.

I loved living in Denver, I loved the view, the air. I even loved the insane weather that never made any sense. I lived in a suburb like most people who drove into the city, not downtown, but I didn't even mind the commute. When I had lived on the east side of town, I had been able to take the light rail in, but the west side of town didn't have everything I needed yet. But they were working on it, *so they said.*

I let out a deep breath. I spent so much time these days trying to live in my head rather than in the reality of the job I hated. So focusing on the commute and my family meant I didn't dwell on the day-to-day life that was slowly sucking the life from me.

Everything was fine. I loved this.

I loved my job.

The fact that I kept having to say that worried me, but it was a dream job. I sort of made it up as I went along and excelled in a business that stressed me out—when they powers that be allowed me.

And now I was meeting with my boss's rival. This was going to go lovely.

But he didn't know who I was. Unless he googled my number like I should have done this whole time. That seemed like a very big lapse in judgment.

I walked the two blocks toward the center of town, and finally made my way to the main street that I loved. There were little cafés and small businesses everywhere. Nothing looked too commercialized or downtrodden. People seemed to like each other on this particular street. It was always surprising since most of the time people tended to ignore each other.

Taboo had been located here since before I started working, and probably years before that. I loved the coffee and the pastries and needed to come down here for sandwiches more often, but I ate at my desk more than I should.

I looked down at my gray pants and soft pink top, and realized I looked like a business professional, not someone off to get afternoon coffee with a man I didn't even know.

Except for the fact I knew his name and what he looked like.

This was insane.

"Get over it, Blakely. It's a cup of coffee," I muttered to myself before opening the door to walk in.

There could have been tables around or even cute decorations. There could have been a thousand people in there, begging for coffee and pastries, but I didn't see them.

Instead, I only saw him.

Aston Cage.

All six-foot-something of him in a dark gray suit that fit him to a tee. Clearly bespoke or tailored perfectly for him. His piercing blue eyes caught me in a web, and I couldn't stop looking at him.

He was built, broad shouldered, but it narrowed down at the waist, so almost like a swimmer's body. His hair was dark, longer on the top than the sides, and perfectly coiffed as if he spent far too long in the mirror.

Or maybe he just woke up like that. Perfect and amazing.

Somebody bumped into me, and I moved to the side, realizing that I was blocking the door.

"I'm sorry."

"It's okay. If I had someone looking at me like that, I'd stand there too," the stranger said before she waved her fingers at me and him and moved back.

I moved to the side then, as Aston came forward.

"Hi," I whispered.

"Hi," he said right back, his voice deep, intoxicating.

What was with this? We hadn't even said anything.

When his lips quirked into a smile, I blinked, telling myself to snap out of it.

"I see you also Googled me," he said softly.

"I'm sorry. Hi, I'm Blakely," I said, awkwardly holding out my hand.

Aston looked down at it, that smile still on his face, and slid his hand over mine. "Aston. Can I get you a cup of coffee?"

"That would be lovely," I said with a laugh, and

then he did the silliest and most attractive thing ever, and lifted my hand to his lips, and I knew there was a problem.

"Oh wow," another woman said as she walked by, fanning herself.

I blushed and took my hand back. "Now that I'm done making a scene. I'd love coffee. Though I am more of a latte girl."

"We can do a latte."

"Should I ask if you do this often? I feel like I should ask if you do this often."

"I have never asked a wrong number out for coffee before. Though I have been here before. Not with another woman though."

"Oh. That's good."

"It is."

We ordered our coffees, talking of weather and sports like we were good at, and I had to wonder if we would talk about anything else.

But it was just coffee after all.

The place was full, so we ended up sitting outside at a little table, nerves running through me.

"So. I would ask what you do, but I sort of know what you do."

"My brother who works in security would probably want to know if you knew that before you Googled me."

I blinked. "As in I somehow entered myself into your life through a random text message? Like I'm the one who typed it in?"

"That's what he would want to know. I assumed that you didn't somehow secretly break into my other brother's house to type in your phone number."

My lips quirked, my shoulders immediately relaxing.

"Yes, it was all an accident. And I actually didn't Google your name until this morning."

Heat crossed my cheeks, and Aston leaned back and blinked at me. "Really? So you didn't know my name this whole time?"

"It was an oversight. But you didn't ask why."

"Because I Googled you that day," he mumbled, looking a little contrite. "Should I have waited?"

"No, you were the smarter one. Plus, you know, you have the whole family business you need to protect. But I'm not going to be a danger to any of that."

Though I did work for a man who hated him. However, that wasn't going to be a problem. This was just coffee, and Mr. Howard didn't care. They ran in different circles after all.

"I feel like I really should have asked your name."

"Maybe, but it was fun figuring out who you were just through text messages. I mean, I know that you don't like the Penguins."

I rolled my eyes. "I don't not like them. But you have to have loyalty. You're from here."

"I am. But sometimes I travel. And I can't get to an Avs game. Or a Broncos game."

"That is true. And honestly, I have no idea how you even got time away to have lunch today. You have to be too busy to have coffee today. What I know of your business is insane. You guys do so much."

He shrugged, tapping his finger on his mug. "True, and I have a good team and family that works with me. However, I'm allowed to have coffee with a beautiful woman."

I rolled my eyes. "That's a lie."

"It is not. I'm sorry to say, but you are beautiful."

"Well, I could say the same to you, but I'm pretty sure the two women that literally swooned next to you while we were talking in there answered that for both of us."

He snorted and finished his coffee. "I can't say that happens often."

"No you just don't notice it."

"So you didn't notice the man looking at you?"

"I only noticed you." I put my hand over my mouth and groaned. "Pretend I didn't say that."

"If it helps, I hadn't even realized I was standing there gawking at you until that woman said something," he whispered.

"Oh."

Oh.

"I really have to go back to work," I said after a moment, and he nodded.

"Same. I have meetings. But I'd like to do this again?"

My cheeks warmed. "Coffee in the middle of a workday?"

"Or dinner."

"Dinner. Dinner could be good."

He stood up and took my hand. "I'll text you?" he asked, the light in his eyes dancing.

I wanted to know this man. This enigma. "Okay. Text me." Texting him felt familiar in such an unfamiliar situation.

He kissed my hand again, and I rolled my eyes.

"I'm sorry, I've never met someone who actually did that."

"I don't think I've ever actually done that," he said, squeezing my hand. "It just felt apropos."

"I'm busy this weekend," I blurted. "But maybe next weekend?"

"Next weekend can work, and as it happens, I'm busy as well."

"Well, this was nice, I'll talk to you soon?" I asked, knowing I was babbling at this point.

"Yes, Blakely, I'll talk to you soon. It was lovely to meet you in person. Especially for a wrong number." And then he walked away, and I did my best not to watch him do so.

Oh, I was in so much trouble.

"I cannot believe I'm back here at your house helping you choose what to wear. I don't think we've ever done that and yet here I am. Again."

I rolled my eyes at Isabella before taking a long look in the mirror. I wore a coral pink dress that had pockets and flared a bit. I was comfortable and it was one of my favorites, but it went to my knees, and looked a little too casual.

Isabella studied me in the mirror and tilted her head. "This is more of a sundress, right?"

"Not quite a sundress, but maybe like a day dress in the spring?"

She smiled. "And on a quiet first date in high school."

"Okay, so this dress is a no."

I quickly stripped out of my dress, and without even offering, Isabella took it from me. She immediately hung it up, and I picked up the next one.

"Okay, this one should work." It was a light blue chiffon sort of dress that went to my ankles, with a high slit. It had this lacy overlay that looked a little bit like tulle but really wasn't. The one strap was thin around my neck, and the other one was thick and made a bow at the neck.

"Is that a bridesmaid's dress?" Isabella asked.

I flushed, realizing I looked like Cinderella on a bender in this outfit.

"Yes. They make you buy these things and then say you can wear them again. But when can I wear this again? Do you see how much tulle-like fabric this has?" I asked, fluffing at the bow.

"I bet you my sister could fix it."

"She could?" I asked, eager.

"Of course. She's had to sew her costumes all the time. However, your gala is tonight. I don't think she's going to be able to rescue this in a few hours. Maybe for another event. Lord knows you go to enough of them."

I sighed and then stripped off the dress, getting tangled in the extra bow, and was grateful when Isabella turned her face from me so I couldn't see her laugh. "This isn't funny. I'm panicking."

"Don't panic. You have plenty of time."

I raised a brow and then looked at the clock on my bedside table. "I have three hours. Three hours to shower, figure out what I'm supposed to do with my hair, do my makeup, and make sure that I have the right shoes and bag for this. I don't think three hours is enough."

"Yes, because you're such an old hag it's going to take you forever."

"Thank you for understanding my pleas."

"Blakely, my best friend. You're going to be fine. You have so many dresses in here. We'll find you something. And I brought you a few as well."

"And I'm grateful. But I don't think my boobs are going to fit in it."

"Are you calling me small-chested?" Isabella asked, in her most prim of ice queen voices.

To most people Isabella was standoffish, a little rude, and very much protective of her family. She was literally called the ice queen by people at her job, and straight to her face. They didn't even bother to whisper the nicknames behind her back. However, my best friend reveled in it. Because it kept people at a safe distance, and they treated her with respect at work. Maybe a little fear, maybe a little reverence, but respect.

I didn't mind that about her and found it more real and endearing than anything.

"Okay, what about this one?" I asked, picking up an A-line sage green dress.

"No. The slit's too high and I think there's a stain on it."

"Damn it. I thought I went to the dry cleaners with this. Maybe I forgot?"

"Maybe. You are busier than me most days."

I crossed my eyes, a little annoyed. "I have to remind myself that I like my job. But some days it's so hard."

"You don't like your job, you like what you're doing, and you just don't like the place of business. Hence why you had to work late today even though your boss wasn't there, and everyone's expecting you to be there tonight. All dressed up and fancy-free."

"What does fancy-free mean?" I asked, staring at her in the mirror as I held up my stained sage dress.

"I'm not sure. Let me look it up."

"Oh good. We can get lost in this. We can forget that I have to meet with humans tonight."

"You're great meeting with humans. I mean,

you're always so personable, and everyone likes seeing you. Don't stress. You've got this."

"I have to go and schmooze so that way the boss can get more clients."

"That's what these events are for. But you've got this. We'll find you something to wear. You're beautiful, you have things to work with, and like I said, you're not too much of an old hag."

"Seriously, the love that I feel from you? I don't think I can hold back my yearning."

"One day we'll finally take each other wildly in the barn and no one will know our secrets."

We met gazes, before each bursting out in laughter, and she handed me a soft pink dress.

"What's this one?" I asked.

"It's mine. And it might not fit you in the boobs, mostly because you have a lot more than me."

"You're no slack there," I teased.

"You can talk all about them in the barn later," she whispered, wiggling her eyebrows.

"It's beautiful," I whispered, holding up the soft pink dress that would flow down to my ankles, barely brushing the floor if I wore the right heels.

"I've never seen you in this."

"I bought it for an event I never went to. So it's just been sitting in my closet. I should have given it to one of my sisters, since I figured they would wear it more than me, but I just haven't. So I get to give it to you. My other sister."

"Calling me your sister after saying you'll take me in the barn adds a whole new level to our fan fiction."

She cringed and gestured for me to try it on. "Let's see how it is on you. Hag."

I flipped her off, even as I began to slide on the dress. It fit perfectly in the waist, a heart-shaped neckline that accentuated my breasts. It had tiny straps that held the dress up and for that I was grateful.

"Well, it seems the dress was meant for you," she whispered.

I met her gaze in the mirror and swallowed hard. "It's gorgeous. But I don't want to take away the first time you ever wear it."

"It didn't look as good on me. We have different coloring. Honestly now, it should just be yours. I might take the sage green dress though. And see if I can get out the stain."

"You don't have to do that."

"It's my nemesis. Now, go take off that dress, and take a shower."

"Aw, I thought you were asking me to take off the dress for other reasons."

"We do not have time to learn all about our hidden places, Blakely. We have to get you ready for a gala. So do you think Mr. Cage will be there?"

I tripped over my own two feet, and she raised a brow at me, and I shook my head. "I'm sure *a* Cage will be there. His family does own one of the largest corporations in the city."

"I don't know too much about them, to be honest."

"Well they run in my circles. Or at least, in my boss's circles. And he hates them."

"Really?"

"I don't know why. But he always gets annoyingly growly about them, and he wants to beat them."

"So I take it you're not going to do lunch with him when he asks officially? Or dinner?"

"My boss or Aston?"

Isabella snorted. "Yes, Aston."

"I don't know. He's only texted a hello, but we've been busy. Nothing more."

"Well that's not fun."

"We have lives." I tried not to let the disappointment pepper my tone. He had said that he was busy all weekend, and so was I. Hence this event. It wasn't like I wanted to continue to flirt over texts with him. I didn't even know if I was going to go out with him. Although it had already come up as something we were going to do. A week from now.

"Well, just have fun. And what will you do if he is there though?" she asked, her voice soft as I stripped and got into the shower. I let the hot water run over my body as I thought about what I would do, and I didn't have an answer. That should have worried me more than anything.

"I'll say hello and be cordial. But this is a work event."

"So socializing with the Cages isn't in your repertoire?"

I washed my hair quickly, looking for more answers. "He probably won't even be there."

"If he was, would he bring a date?"

I nearly slipped in the shower, and glared at her as I looked around my shower curtain. "Really?"

She winced. "Sorry. I'm in a weird mood."

"Are you okay?" I asked, worried.

She waved me off and smiled. "I'm just fine. Promise. We were talking about you. If he's there, you should dance. You said there was a spark."

"And my boss would absolutely hate it."

"So a win-win," she teased.

I shook my head. "Not so much if I want to keep my job."

"He can't fire you for flirting with a Cage."

"I'm sure he'd find a way about competing interests, or just any other way. He's not a nice man." My contract was year by year and though I was one of his best employees, I also outshone some of his "Yes Men" on occasion. I stood up to him, but there were always company politics. Therefore we had a dance and charity gala this evening. None of the others on staff were required to go. But the boss wanted to show off his employee in a dress so he could show the world how modern he was. Oh, he'd never say that, and no one would never outright point it out—but we all knew it was the case.

"Then why do you work for him?"

That was the question. And I wish I had better answers. "Because it's the best job I can get. And I'm sure a Cage will be there, but it's not going to be him. It's going to be one of his countless brothers."

"Okay, let's hope it's that way so you don't have to make a choice. At least in front of everyone."

I rinsed the conditioner out of my hair. "Nothing's ever easy."

"No. But that's life. Unending pain and suffering until you die."

I toweled off my hair, pausing to stare at her. "Is everything okay, Isabelle?" I asked, worry etched in my tone. "We don't have to talk about me all the time."

"I'm perfectly fine. I'm just razzing you. Now, let's get your hair done. And you know we talk about my family more often than not."

"Are you sure you have time for this?"

"I have time to help my best friend look hot in a dress for whoever might show up."

"He's not going to be there," I warned.

"Fine, I have time to help my friend look hot in a dress for herself. How about that?"

"Yes. Let's go with that."

It took an hour, but drying my hair, straightening it so I could curl it, and then doing a full face of makeup took time. Thankfully I had my grandmother's jewelry that I could make work with the dress, and when I finished the final clasp on my bracelet, I sighed in the mirror.

"Well, I don't look too shabby."

"You look beautiful. And don't stain my dress."

"I thought that I was being gifted this and you were taking the sage one?"

She smiled far too sweetly. "No, I'm just fixing the stain, and we can share both dresses. How about that?"

"You are a riot."

"I try. Now go knock them dead."

"Or at least try to win over clients. All in the name of finance," I said, sighing when Isabella rolled her eyes at me.

I drove myself to the event, because I was planning on only having one glass of champagne if that. I didn't want to deal with a ride-share or wait on anyone else. Thankfully there was a valet at the hotel, so I didn't have to find a way to park in this dress.

Holding my small clutch, I made my way into the hotel ballroom, smiling at a few people as I made my way around the room.

I saw a few familiar faces, though it was mostly strangers. When I caught the eyes of my boss's wife, she smiled softly at me and waved. I did not know how that sweet woman was married to that monster of a man, but then again, maybe he was only an asshole at work, and saved all his goodness for home.

The boss in question gave me a once-over and a tight nod, and I figured I'd passed some test.

A waiter passed by with a glass of champagne, and I milled about, holding my drink, barely taking a sip, and speaking with potential clients. I had already done research on the people that I knew I should talk to at the gala, the ones who had RSVP'd. But I hadn't seen a Cage on the list. Mostly because they were always invited, and they didn't have to RSVP to things like this.

That wasn't ominous at all.

"Well, small world."

It indeed was a small world. My hand squeezed on the stem of my champagne flute, and I turned around slowly, to stare into the eyes of Aston Cage.

"Oh. You're here."

He tilted his head and gave me that smile. The one that made my thighs clench, and I had to count backward from ten so I could catch my breath. "Yes, I'm here. The foundation is one that's close to my mother's heart. So we take turns attending different events. And it's my turn. Fancy that."

"I didn't know you'd be here."

He raised a brow. "And I didn't know you'd be here."

"Is it okay?" I shook my head. "Of course it's okay. This is work."

"You work for Howard, don't you?" he asked,

his voice low. People really weren't paying attention to us other than the fact that their gazes would catch on Aston's. Because that's what the Cages did. They pulled in attention even when they weren't trying.

"I do."

"Is that going to be a problem?" he asked.

"Is what going to be a problem?" I asked, purposely obtuse. It wasn't as if we were making promises to each other or doing anything. I was just standing and speaking to a man at a gala, with a respectable distance between us. That's all that needed to be said.

"Well then, I'm glad that I'm the one who came, and not James."

"Which one was James on the text?" I asked, teasing.

"Probably the one trying to order us all."

"Wouldn't that be you?" I asked.

"That's what James would say," he replied, laughter in his gaze. Then a small pause. "Dance with me, Blakely," he whispered.

I shook my head. "I really shouldn't."

"There's many people on the dance floor, you can say you are schmoozing me."

"I don't think my boss would like that."

"Well, you should dance with me anyway. Please? I don't want to wait for a dinner date."

I couldn't see my boss anywhere, but I knew that this would probably get out. Because everything with the Cages did.

I set down my champagne flute on the table next to me anyway and placed my now free hand in his open one.

"Okay."

"Good." He clasped his hand over mine, and I was lost.

Getting hard in the middle of a ballroom while standing near many of my trustees, backers, and business rivals probably wasn't the best idea. But as soon as I saw Blakely across the dance floor, everything in me shifted.

And it wasn't just her beauty—those sharp cheekbones, those light eyes that shone underneath the soft lighting of the room. She'd even put her hair up in a half-do thing, so it framed her face, but still looked elegant. I used to be better about knowing what those were called, or even what kind of dress she wore. It had been a long time since I had been with anyone for that matter.

But no, it wasn't any of what she looked like, it was the aura that seemed to surround her and others could feel it too. She may not have even realized they did. They stopped what they were doing to glance over at her, as if they wanted to know her. She'd catch everyone's attention, whether it be to judge her or to admire her.

Or in my case, to barely hold back from falling down on my knees in front of her.

And now she was mine. If only for this dance.

"So, I didn't realize this is what you would be doing this weekend," she said softly as we glided across the dance floor. She had her hand on my arm, her other clasping my own, and I smiled down at her.

I hadn't done this much smiling since my brother's wedding when they had all danced and partied and looked as if they actually were going to have a great time.

It was a little odd to think I was doing so now.

"We try to represent the family."

"Are you the only one here?"

I shook my head before I looked over hers to see both of my brothers raising their brows. Flynn and James had curious expressions on their faces, nearly identical even though neither one of them were the twins.

It must be odd to see me dancing with someone

since I usually did not dance at these things. I smiled, spoke to those I needed to, did a speech if required, and wrote a check. I never got out on the dance floor when I came alone.

And yet here I was, with Blakely, losing my mind.

"Two of my brothers are here, they're behind you, staring at me and wondering why I'm dancing."

"You don't dance? You seem to be good at it."

The heat of her seared me through her dress and my tuxedo, and I had to swallow hard not to do anything that would shame us both. "I don't dance. I can, but I don't."

"Then why with me?" she asked, her voice a little breathy.

"I think you know, Blakely."

"So how many brothers do you have here?" she asked, changing the subject. I didn't mind, both of us needed to take a step to breathe if the way that her pulse fluttered against her neck was any indication.

"James and Flynn are here because it was our turn. My parents are out of town, or my mother and father would be here. Mother enjoys attending these events."

I hoped the bite wasn't in my tone at that,

considering she liked all of her sons at these things so she could show us off.

"So three of you. That's a good number then."

I shook my head as I twirled her during the next song, both of us not having realized the song had even changed. "It's not even a full fifty percent. There are a lot of us."

"I knew you had a few brothers, but I hadn't really paid attention too much beyond that."

"There's more than a few of us. Not all of us work with Cage Enterprises though. However we do all have a stake in the company because it's our family. If that makes sense."

"Not in the slightest," she said with a laugh, her eyes shining.

"Understandable. We are here as a family to show our support, to donate, and to do what our family requires."

"I would say that sounds annoying, but you get to eat some decent food, and probably make business deals along the way."

I raised a brow at her but nodded. "Yes. That is always a perk. What about you? You're here with Howard Enterprises?"

I could feel eyes on me, and I knew it wasn't just those who were curious who I was dancing with.

No, the proprietor of Howard Enterprises was probably not happy about the woman who worked for him dancing in my arms. But there was nothing I could do about that. Nothing I wanted to do about that.

"Yes. Dancing with you is probably a mistake."

"He doesn't hate me that much, does he?" I asked, honestly curious.

"No. I don't think so. I think he just wants to one-up you."

"So does you dancing with me have anything to do with that?" I asked, oddly curious.

Her eyes narrowed, and she stopped dancing. I cursed under my breath and was grateful we were at the edge of the dance floor.

"I'm sorry. I didn't mean that."

"No you did. He didn't *ask* me to dance with you. You're the one who asked me to dance. And I knew it was going to be a mistake. He wants to beat you in everything all the time. So me dancing with the enemy probably isn't a good idea."

"I'm the enemy, am I?" I asked, my voice low.

She swallowed hard and shook her head. "No. It's not so dramatic as that."

"Good."

I lifted her hand up to my lips and kissed it

again, a bare brush of my mouth against her skin, and her intake of breath was all I needed to hear.

"You need to stop doing that."

"I don't know if I want to."

Nobody was paying attention to us now, as the emcee was making their rounds, so I tugged on her hand and pulled her around the corner.

"Aston," she said with a laugh, and I did what I had been wanting to do since I first saw her. I pressed my lips to hers.

She didn't pull away, didn't freeze. Instead wrapped her fingers under the lapels of my jacket and pulled me closer.

Groaning, I deepened the kiss, my tongue sliding along hers.

"We need to stop. Someone can come around the corner at any minute."

"I'll stop. Soon." I kissed her again, needing her taste, craving her, and when I knew that it would be too much if I continued, I wrenched myself away, my chest rising and falling in deep pants.

"Holy hell," I growled.

"Oh."

I looked over at Blakely, her hand over her bruised lips, her eyes wide. "Are you okay? Did I hurt you?"

"Not at all. I don't think I've ever been kissed like that before. Which probably isn't something I should say." I had barely any control when it came to her.

I felt like a cat who caught the canary, and a smile slid across my face. "That sounds like a compliment."

"Maybe. Or maybe I need to get out more." She grinned up at me.

Her eyes danced, and I wanted to know more. I wanted to know everything.

Who was this woman? And why did she do this to me?

"Sorry to interrupt, but they need you." I cursed at Flynn's timing, and Blakely's face drained of color, while she tried to hide behind a potted palm.

"It's just my brother. Everything's fine."

"I'm so embarrassed. I'm *working* for God's sake."

"It's okay, nobody saw. James and I had the exits covered."

"Should it worry me that it sounds like you guys have a plan for this sort of thing?" she asked, slight frost in her tone.

I cursed my brothers and everything they stood for, while I glared at him and James who walked up from behind him. "No, this is new. But we protect our family."

Flynn looked over my shoulder and winked at Blakely. "I'm Flynn. The quiet one here is James. It's good to see you."

"Hi. I'm going to go fix my face. And then I have to...work."

"You look wonderful," James said softly, and I glared at him before turning my back to them and looking at Blakely.

"I have to go be The Cage," I said with a roll of my eyes.

"I love the title." I heard the humor in her tone—even above the slight panic.

"I don't," I said softly. "I want to see you again."

Her eyes widened marginally. "Okay. Maybe not in the middle of a hallway?"

"No. Let's not. I'll call you."

When she let out a soft laugh, I relaxed. Marginally. "Good. And then I'll have my wits about me."

"I need to go." Long before this.

"He really does," Flynn called out.

"Then go," she whispered.

And then I pressed my lips to hers again before letting her walk away, presumably to go fix the blush of her face. But I thought she looked gorgeous.

"So, have you lost your mind?" Flynn asked as we stepped out of earshot.

"Stop it. I don't want to hear it."

Flynn clucked his tongue. "I think you've lost your mind."

"I think you're more like Dorian than we thought," James whispered, and I flipped them both off, before straightening my jacket.

"Let's go be Cages and do what we need to."

"So that's the girl from the chat?" James asked.

I nodded tightly. "We're done here."

"Oh, I think you've just begun," Flynn said with a laugh.

I rolled my eyes at my two brothers, and moved toward the ballroom, knowing we had people to meet, and there was work to be done. My phone buzzed in my pocket however, and I couldn't help but hope it was her.

However it wasn't Blakely calling, it was my mother.

"Answer it, or we're all going to have to deal with that," Flynn said with a roll of his eyes.

I sighed but answered anyway. "Hello, Mother. You're missing a great gala."

"Aston. It's your father."

Ice slid up my spine, and I swallowed hard. I

must have looked as if something was wrong, because both my brothers stopped teasing me, and stood still, staring at me.

"What's wrong?"

"Your father is dead. And I need you here. Call the others. We need you." She hung up without saying anything else, and I stared at my brothers knowing everything had changed.

He hadn't called.

He should have called. But he hadn't.

I waited by my phone for four days, waiting for a call. The weekend had passed, and then the holiday where there was no work, just me waiting by a phone as I sat at home alone.

But he hadn't called.

I had picked up my phone countless times to call him, but he had said he would call me. And he was Aston Cage, man of business. I wasn't going to be the one who called first. Right?

Phone in hand, I knew I just needed to put on my big-girl panties and do it. I looked up his texts, pressed his icon, and called.

It rang once and went straight to voicemail. I frowned but didn't leave a message.

He had sent me straight to voicemail. Maybe he was in a meeting? Or maybe he just wasn't calling.

I knew I needed to get to work, and I had to stop stressing over the fact that a man hadn't called me after he had kissed the daylights out of me in the middle of a work function.

That was so unprofessional it wasn't even funny. I had gone right back to work, spoken to the clients I needed to, and made a few business deals for my boss. I had done what I was supposed to do, and yet everything felt different.

I felt different.

I sighed and went to finish my breakfast as I turned on the morning news. I needed to leave soon so I wouldn't be late, but everything felt off.

This just in, Dorian Cage the patriarch of the Cage family is dead at age sixty. He was the former president of Cage Enterprises and Businesses, a worldwide and billion-dollar firm of real estate development, small business backers, environmental research, including dozens of other subsidiaries. And while he wasn't at the helm of the business at the time of his death, with his eldest son Aston Cage taking that position, he was still the man on the mountain for many. However it seems that his death, while of natural causes, did not come without a scandal of its own.

There's more to come on this once we have all of the information, but according to inside sources, the Cage family has its secrets.

Everything froze within me as I stared at the TV and tried to understand what I was hearing.

Aston's father was dead.

No wonder he couldn't call or text. His father was dead.

And a scandal? I didn't even want to know exactly what that was, but I couldn't even imagine.

I picked up my phone again and knew that he was far too busy for me, but I needed to text. Needed to say something. Anything.

ME:

I'm so sorry, Aston. I can't imagine your loss. My thoughts are with you and your family. And if there's anything you need from me, ever, let me know. I'm sorry.

I sent the text, hoping it was enough, even though it would never be. Maybe he would see it and remember. But I was just the girl from the texts, a woman that he saw on the dance floor and kissed.

No wonder he hadn't called.

Tears pricked my eyes, as emotions washed over me, but I knew that it was silly.

This wasn't about me. He had the most obvious reason not to call.

I gathered my things and headed to work, and knew that I was going to have to find a way to either get over Aston Cage, or make sure he wasn't alone. Because from what I could tell, as the eldest, he had the weight of the world on his shoulders.

Or maybe I was thinking too hard, and I had nothing to do with it. It was all just a dream. Before I knew who he was.

I walked into work, and I realized that people were staring at me. It was odd, to feel the weight of a thousand stares, but I ignored them, and made my way to my desk.

"Blakely, come inside my office," Mr. Howard ordered, his voice deep, commanding. Ice slid down my back, but I swallowed hard, sitting my bag on the table, and wondering why he was here so early, and why he could want me first thing.

I lifted my chin, and ignored the stares of others, as I made my way to his office.

"Hello, Mr. Howard, good morning. What can I do for you?"

"You're fired."

I blinked at him, caught off guard. "What?"

"You're fired for working with the competition. We lost the Meridian account to the Cages, and that happened right after your little dance with him. We can connect the dots and have done so."

I schooled my features, hoping my racing heart didn't beat out of my chest. "What? I have nothing to do with that."

"Oh? So it's just a coincidence that we lost the biggest account that we have to the Cages right after you went on a little dance break and whatever else with the head of the company? What else did you say when you were sleeping with him?" he spat before his lawyer shut him up.

Rage filled me, as bile crept up my throat. "I didn't do anything..."

"We have evidence to say different," one of the lawyers said, and I glared at him, and realized that they were going to find any reason to get me out. They were going to lie and twist the narrative, and I wouldn't be able to fight back. I could sue. I could plead my case. And yet no one would listen to me.

Because I had danced with Aston Cage, and I had apparently made a fool of my boss.

"I didn't do this," I repeated.

"And I don't believe you," Mr. Howard said before gesturing to his lawyers and security to escort me out.

People continued to stare, as I realized this was my reality.

I had made one mistake—dancing with a gorgeous man who made me smile.

And even though I could find my own lawyers, and I could find a way to get out of a wrongful termination suit, they would find another way to push me out.

Out of a job I hated—out of a job that broke me.

And somehow this was Aston Cage's fault.

Because this was before I knew. Before I knew him. Before I knew how much I could feel.

And before I knew how much I could break.

Aston Cage was out of my life. Only the scars of that one dance with a Cage would shroud my life and my future.

I hoped he never called.

I had made enough mistakes when it came to Aston Cage.

And I would never make them again.

Start the Cage Family series and find out what happens with Aston and Blakely in:
The Forever Rule

Start the Cage Family series and find out what happens with Aston and Blakely in:
The Forever Rule

A NOTE FROM CARRIE ANN RYAN

Thank you so much for reading **CARELESS.**

You don't have to wait long to read all of Callum & Felicity's romance!

The Ashford Creek series is quickly becoming one of my favorites. I truly cannot wait to dive deeper into this town and these families.

Yes, each Ashford is getting a book.

But they aren't all.

And yes...I have secrets too.

If you'd like to read Briar's story, you can find it in Pieces of Me!

Ashford Creek

Book 1: Legacy (Callum & Felicity)

Book 2: Crossroads (Bohdi & Keira)

Book 3: Westward (Atlas & Elizabeth)

Don't miss the next Ashford Creek romance with Kiera & Bodhi in Crossroads.

And if you'd like to read a bonus scene, you can find it **HERE**.

If you want to make sure you know what's coming next from me, you can sign up for my newsletter at www.CarrieAnnRyan.com; follow me on twitter at @CarrieAnnRyan, or like my Facebook page. I also have a Facebook Fan Club where we have trivia, chats, and other goodies. You guys are the reason I get to do what I do and I thank you.

Make sure you're signed up for my MAILING LIST so you can know when the next releases are available as well as find giveaways and FREE READS.

Happy Reading!

FROM THE FOREVER RULE
ASTON

*The Cages are the most prestigious
family in Denver—at least according to the
patriarch of the Cage Family.
And the Cages have rules.
Rules only they know.*

I always knew that one day my father would die. I hadn't realized that day would come so soon. Or that the last words I would say to him would've been in anger.

I had been having one of the best nights of my life, a beautiful woman in my arms, and a smile on my face when I received the phone call that had changed my family's life.

The fact that I had been smiling had been a shock, because according to my brothers, I didn't smile much. I was far too busy being *The Cage* of Cage Enterprises.

We were a dominant force in the city of Denver when it came to certain real estate ventures, as well as being one of the only ethical and environmentally friendly ones who tried to keep up with that. We had our hands in countless different pots around the world, but mostly we gravitated in the state of Colorado—our home.

I had not created the company, no, that honor had gone to my grandfather, and then my father. The Cage Enterprises were and would always be a family endeavor. And when my father had stepped away a few years ago, stating he had wanted to see the world, and also see if his sons could actually take up the mantle, I had stepped in—not that the man believed we could.

My brothers were in various roles within the company, at least those who had wanted to be part of it. But I was the face of Cage Enterprises.

So no, I hadn't smiled often. There wasn't time. We weren't billionaires with mega yachts. We worked seventy-hour weeks to make sure *all* our employees had a livable wage while wining and dining with those who looked down at us for not being on their level. And others thought we were the high and mighty anyway since they didn't understand us. So, I didn't smile.

But I had smiled that night.

It had been a gala for some charity, one I couldn't even remember off the top of my head. We had donated between the company and my own finances—we always did. But I couldn't even remember anything about why we were there.

Yet I could remember her smile. The heat in her eyes when she had looked up at me, the feel of her body pressed against mine as we had danced along the dance floor, and then when we ended up in the hallway, bodies pressed against one another, needing each other, wanting each other.

And I had put aside all my usual concepts of business and life to have this woman in my arms.

And then my mother had called and had shattered that illusion.

"Your father is dead."

She hadn't even braced me for the blow. A heart attack on a vacation on a beach in Majorca, and he was dead. She hadn't cried, hadn't said anything, just told me that I had to be the one to tell my brothers.

And so, I had, all six of them. Because of course Loren Cage would have seven sons. He couldn't do things just once, he had to make sure he left his legacy, his destiny.

And that was why we were here today, in a high-rise in Centennial, waiting on my father's lawyer to show up with the reading of the will.

"Hey, when is Winstone going to get here?" Dorian asked, his typical high energy playing on his face, and how he tapped his fingers along the hand-carved wooden table.

I stared at my brother, at those piercing blue eyes that matched my own, and frowned. He should be here soon. He did call us all here after all."

"I still don't know why we all had to be here for the reading of the will," Hudson whispered as he stared off into the distance. Neither Dorian nor Hudson worked for Cage Enterprises. They had stock with the company, and a few other connections because that's what family did, but they didn't work on the same floors as some of us and hadn't been elbow to elbow with our father before he had retired. Though dear old dad had worked in our small town more often than not in the end. In fact, Hudson didn't even live in Denver anymore. He had moved to the town we owned in the mountains.

Because of course we Cages owned a damned town. Part of me wasn't sure if the concept of having our name on everything within the town had been on purpose or had occurred organically. Though knowing my grandfather, perhaps it had been exactly what he'd wanted. He had bought up a few buildings, built a few more, and now we owned three-quarters of the town, including the major resort which brought in tourists and income.

And that was why we were here.

"You have to be here because you're evidently in the will," I said softly, trying not to get annoyed that we were waiting for our father's lawyer. Again.

"You would think he would be able to just send us a memo. I mean, it should be clear right? We all know what stakes we have in, we should just be able to do things evenly," Theo said, his gaze off into the distance. My younger brother also didn't work for the company, instead he had decided to go to culinary school, something my father had hated. But you couldn't control a Cage, that was sort of our deal.

"Why would you be cut out of the will?" I asked, honestly curious.

"Because I married a man and a woman," he drawled out. "You know he hasn't spoken to me since before the wedding," Ford said, and I saw the hurt in his gaze even though I knew he was probably trying to hide it.

"Well, he was an asshole, what do you expect?" James asked.

I looked behind Ford to see my brother and co-chair of Cage Enterprises standing with his hands in his pockets, staring out the window.

With Flynn, our vice president, standing beside him, they looked like the heads of businesses they were. While they wore suits and so did I, we were the only ones.

Dorian and Hudson were both in jeans, Hudson's having a hole at the knee. And probably not as a fashion statement, most likely because it had torn at some point, and he hadn't bothered to buy another pair. Theo was in slacks, but a Henley with his sleeves pushed up, tapping his finger just like Hudson, clearly wanting to get out of here as well. Ford had on cargo pants, and a tight black T-shirt, and looked like he had just gotten off his shift.

He owned a security company with his husband and a few other friends, and did security for the Cages when he could, though I knew he didn't like to work with family often. And I knew it wasn't because of us. No, it was Father—even if he had officially *retired*. It was always Father.

And he was gone.

"Can't believe the asshole's gone," I whispered.

Ford's brows rose. "Look at that, you calling him an asshole. I'm proud."

"You should show him respect," Mother said as she came inside the room, her high heels tapping against the marble floors. I didn't bother standing up like I normally would have, because Melanie Cage looked to be in a *mood*.

She didn't look sad that Dad was gone, more like angry that he would dare go against their plans. What plans? I didn't know, but that was my mother.

She came right up to Dorian and leaned down to kiss his cheek. She didn't even bother to look at the rest of us. Dorian was Mother's favorite. Which I knew Dorian resented, but I didn't have to deal with mommy issues at this moment.

No, we had to deal with father issues at this point.

"I'm going to go get him," Flynn replied, turning toward the door. "I'm really not in the mood to wait any longer, especially since he's being so secretive about this meeting."

As I had been thinking just the same, I nodded at Flynn though he didn't need my permission. However, just then, the door opened, and I frowned when it wasn't just Mr. Winstone walking into the conference room.

I stared as an older woman walked through the door following Mr. Winstone, and four women and another man with messy hair and tattered cut-up jeans that matched Hudson's walked behind them.

The guy looked familiar, as if I'd seen him somewhere, or maybe it was just his eyes.

Where had I seen those eyes before?

"Phoebe? What are you doing here?" Ford asked as he moved forward and gripped the hands of one of the women.

"I was going to ask the same question," Phoebe asked as she looked at Ford, then around the room.

Those of us sitting stood up, confused about why this other family—because they were clearly a family—had decided to enter the room.

"We're here to meet the lawyer about my father's death, Ford. Why would you and the Cages be here?" she asked, and I wondered how the hell Mr. Winstone had fucked up so badly? Why the hell was he letting another family that clearly seemed to be in shock come into our room? This wasn't how he normally handled things.

Ford was the one who answered though—thankfully—because I had no idea what the hell was going on.

"Phoebe, we're here for my dad's will reading. What the hell is going on?" he asked. Phoebe looked around, as well as the others.

I stared at them, at the tall willowy one with wide eyes, at the smaller one with tears still in her eyes as if she was the only one truly mourning, and at the woman who seemed to be in charge, not the mother. Instead she had shrewd eyes and was glaring at all of us. The man stood back, hands in pockets, and looked just as shell-shocked as Ford.

But before Mr. Winstone or anyone else could say anything, my mother spoke in such a crisp, icy tone that I froze.

"I don't know why you're acting so dramatic. You knew your father was an asshole. He just liked creating drama," she snapped.

As I tried to catch up with her words, the older woman answered. "Melanie, stop."

This couldn't be happening. Because things started to click into place. The fact that the man at the other end of this table had our eyes, and that everybody looked so fucking shocked. I didn't know how Ford knew this Phoebe, and I would be getting answers.

"We had a deal," my mother continued, as it seemed that the rest of us were just now catching on. "You would keep your family away from mine. We would share Loren, but I got the name, I got the family. You got whatever else. But now it looks like Loren decided to be an asshole again."

"What are you talking about?" the shrewd sister asked as she came forward, her hands fisted at her side.

"Excuse me," I said, clearing my throat. I was going to be damned if I let anyone else handle this meeting. I was The Cage now. "Will someone please explain?"

"Well, I wasn't quite sure how this was going to work out," Mr. Winstone began, and we all quieted, while I wanted to strangle the man. What did he mean how *the hell this would work out*? What was this?

This seemed like a big fucking mistake.

"Loren Cage had certain provisions in his will for

both of his families. And one of the many require-
ments that I will go over today is that this meeting
must take place." He paused and I hoped it wasn't
for effect, because I was going to throttle him if it
was. "Loren Cage had two families. Seven sons with
his wife Melanie, and four daughters and a son with
his mistress, Constance."

"We went by partner," the other mother
corrected.

I blinked, counting the adults in the room.
"Twelve?" I asked, my voice slightly high-pitched.

"Busy fucking man," Dorian whispered.

Hudson snorted, while we just stood and stared
at each other.

*This could not be happening. A secret family? No, we
were not that cliché.*

"I can't do this," Phoebe blurted, her eyes wide.

"Oh, stop overreacting," my mother scorned.

"Do not talk to my daughter that way." The
other mother glared.

"It was always going to be an issue," Mother
continued. "All the secrets and the lies. And now the
kids will have to deal with it. Because God forbid
Loren ever deal with anything other than his own
dick."

"That's enough," I snapped.

"Don't you dare talk to us like that," the shrewd sister snapped right back.

"I will talk however I damn well please. I am going to need to know exactly how this happened," I shouted over everyone else's words.

Out of the corner of my eye I saw Phoebe run through the door. Ford followed and then the tall willowy one joined.

"Shit," I snapped.

"Language," Mother bit out.

I laughed. "Really? You are going to talk to me about language."

I looked over at James, who shrugged, before he put two fingers in his mouth and whistled that high-pitched whistle that only he could do.

Everyone froze as Theo rubbed his ear and glared at me.

"Winstone," I said through gritted teeth. "I take it we all have to be here in order for this to happen?"

He cleared his throat. "At least a majority. But you all had to at least step into the room."

"Excuse me then," I said.

"You're just going to leave? Just like that?" my mother asked.

I whirled on her. "I'm going to go see if my apparent *family* is okay. Then I'm going to come back and we're going to get answers. Because there is no way that I'm going to leave here without them."

I stormed out the door, and thankfully nobody followed me.

Of course, though, I shouldn't have been too swift with that, as the woman who had to be the eldest sister practically ran to my side, her heels tapping against the marble.

"I'm coming with you."

"That's just fine." I paused, knowing that I wasn't angry at these people. No, my father and apparently our mothers were the ones that had to deal with this. I looked over at the woman who Mr. Winstone and the mothers had claimed was my sister and cleared my throat.

"I'm Aston."

"Is this really the time for introductions?" she asked.

"I'm about to go see your sister and my brother to make sure that they're fine, so sure. I would like to know the name of the woman that is running next to me right now."

"I'm running, you're walking quickly because you have such long legs."

I snorted, surprised I could even do that.

"I'm Isabella," she replied after a moment.

"I would say nice to meet you Isabella…" I let my voice trail off.

She let out a sharp laugh before shaking her head. "I'm going to need a moment to wrap my head around this, but not now."

"Same."

We stormed out of the building, and I lagged behind since Ford was standing in front of Phoebe who was in the arms of another man with dark hair and everybody seemed to be talking all at once.

"I just. I can't deal with this right now," Phoebe said, and I realized that something else must have been going on with her right then. She looked tired, and far more emotional than the rest of us.

I looked over at the man holding her and blinked. "Kane?" I asked.

Kane stared at me and let out a breath. "Wow," he said with a laugh.

"We'll handle it," Isabella put in, completely ignoring us. "And if we need to meet again later, we will." Then she looked over at Ford and I, with such menace in her gaze, I nearly took a step back. "Is that a problem?"

I raised my chin, glaring right back at her. "Not at all. However I want answers, so I'd rather not have the meeting canceled right now. But I'm also not going to force any of my," I paused, realization hitting far too hard, "*family* to stay if they don't want to."

And with that, I turned on my heel and went back into the building, with Isabella and Ford following me. Everyone was still yelling in the interim, and I cleared my throat. As Isabella had done it at the same time, everyone paused to look at me.

"Read the damn will. Because we need answers," I ordered Winstone, and he shook like a leaf before nodding.

"Okay. We can do that." He cleared his throat, then he began going over trusts and incomes and buildings and things that I would care about soon, but what I wanted to know was what the hell our father had been thinking about.

"Here's the tricky part," Winstone began, as we all leaned forward, eager to hear what the hell he had to say.

"The family money, not of the business, not of each of your inheritance from other family members, but the bulk of Loren Cage's assets will be split between all twelve kids."

"Are you kidding me?" Isabella asked. "What

money? We weren't exactly poor, but we were solidly middle class."

"We did just fine," the other mother pleaded.

My mother snorted, clearly not believing the words.

I glared at the woman who raised me, willing her to say *anything*. She would probably be pushed out of the window at that point. Not by me, by someone else, but she probably would've earned it.

The lawyer continued. "However to retain the majority of current assets and to keep Cage Lake and all of its subsidiaries you will have to meet as a family once a month for three years. If this does not happen, Cage Enterprises will be broken into multiple parts and sold." He went on into the legalese that I ignored as I tried to hear over the blood pounding in my ears.

"You own a town?" the other man asked.

I looked over at the one man in the room I didn't know the name of. "Not exactly."

"Kyler," Isabella whispered.

In that moment, I realized that I had a brother named Kyler—if this was all to be believed.

"This can't be legal right?" the tall willowy person said.

"Yes Sophia, it can," their mother put in.

Oh good, another sister named Sophia.

Only one name to go. What the hell was wrong with me?

I forced my jaw to relax. "Are you telling us that we need to have all twelve of us at dinner once a month for three years in order to keep what is rightly inherited to us? To keep people in business and keep their jobs?"

"We don't need the money, but everyone else in our employ does," James snapped. "As do those we work with."

"Damn straight," Dorian growled.

"How are we supposed to believe this?" I asked, asking the obvious question.

"First, only five must attend, and two must be of a different family." The lawyer continued as if I hadn't spoken. "Of course you are *all* family…"

"Again, how are we supposed to believe this?" I asked.

"Here are the DNA tests already done."

"Are you fucking kidding me?" Isabella asked.

I looked at her, as she had literally taken the words out of my mouth.

"Isn't that sort of like a violation?" Kyler asked, his face pale.

"We need to get our own lawyers on this," James whispered.

I nodded tightly, knowing we had much more to say on this.

"There's no way this is legal," the youngest said, and I looked over at her.

"What's your name?" I asked.

"Emily. Emily Cage Dixon," she said softly, and we all froze.

"Your middle name is Cage?" I asked, biting out the words.

"All of our middle names are Cage," Sophia said, shaking her head. "I hated it but Dad wanted to be cute because our father's name was Cage Dixon, or maybe it wasn't. Is he also a bigamist?" she asked.

Her mother lifted her chin. "We never married. And no, your father's name was not Dixon, that was my maiden name."

"What?" Sophia asked. "All this time…are our grandparents even dead?"

"Yes, my parents are dead. The same with Loren's." The other mother's eyes filled with tears. "I'm sorry we lied."

"We'll get to that later," Isabella put in, and I was grateful.

I let out a breath. "In order to keep our assets, in

order to keep the family name intact, we need to have *dinner*. For three years."

The small lawyer nodded, his glasses falling down his nose. "At least five of you. And it can start three months after the funeral, which we can plan after this."

"This is ridiculous," Hudson murmured under his breath, before he got up and walked out.

I watched him go, knowing he had his own demons, and tried to understand what the hell was going on. "Why did he do this?" I asked, more to myself than anyone else.

"I never really knew the man, but apparently none of us did," Isabella said, staring off into the distance.

"Leave the paperwork and go," I ordered Winstone, and he didn't even mutter a peep. Instead, he practically ran out of the room. James and Flynn immediately went to the paperwork, and I knew they were scouring it. But from the way that their jaws tightened, I had a feeling that my father had found a way to make this legal. Because we would always have a choice to lose everything. That was the man.

"It's true," my mother put in. "You all share the same father. That was the deal when we got married, and when he decided to bring this other woman into our lives."

"I'm pretty sure you were the other woman," the other mom said.

I pinched the bridge of my nose.

"Stop. All of you." I stared at the group and realized that I was probably the eldest Cage here, other than the moms. I would deal with this. We didn't have a choice. "Whatever happens, we'll deal with it."

"You're in charge now?" Isabella asked, but Sophia shushed her.

I was grateful for that, because I had a feeling Isabella and I were going to butt heads more often than not.

I shrugged, trying to act as if my world hadn't been rocked. "I would say welcome to the Cages, because DNA evidence seems to point that way, however perhaps you were already one of us all along."

Kyler muttered something under his breath I couldn't hear before speaking up. "You have my eyes," he said.

I nodded. "Noticed that too."

The other man tilted his head. "So what, we do dinners and we make nice?"

I sighed. "We don't have to be adversaries."

"You say that as if you're the one in charge," Isabella said again.

"Because he is," Theo said, and they all stared at him.

I tried to tamp down the pride swelling at those words—along with the overwhelming pressure.

Theo continued. "He's the eldest. He's the one that takes care of us. And he's the CEO of Cage Enterprises. He's going to be the one that deals with the paperwork fallout."

"Because family is just paperwork?" Emily asked, her voice lost.

I shook my head. "No, family is insane, and apparently, it's been secret all along. And it looks like we have a few introductions to make, and a few tests to redo. But if it turns out it's true, we're Cages, and we don't back down."

"And what does that mean?" Isabella asked, her tone far too careful.

Theo was the one who finally answered. "It means we're going to have to figure shit out."

And for just an instant, the thought of that beautiful woman with that gorgeous smile came to mind, and I pushed those thoughts away. My family was breaking, or perhaps breaking open. And I didn't have time to worry about things like a woman who had made me smile.

The Cages needed me and after today's meeting there would be no going back to sanity.

Ever.

In the mood to read another family saga? Meet the Cage Family in The Forever Rule!

FROM ONE WAY BACK
TO ME

ELI

When my morning begins with me standing ankle-deep in a basement full of water, I know I probably should have stayed in bed. Only, I was the boss, and I didn't get that choice.

"Hold on. I'm looking for it." East cursed underneath his breath as my younger brother bent down around the pipe, trying his best to turn off the valve. I sighed, waded through the muck in my work boots, and moved to help him. "I said I've got it," East snapped, but I ignored him.

I narrowed my eyes at the evil pipe. "It's old and rusted, and even though it passed an inspection over a year ago, we knew this was going to be a problem."

"And I'm the fucking handyman of this company. I've got this."

"And as a handyman, you need a hand."

"You're hilarious. Seriously. I don't know how I could ever manage without your wit and humor." The dryness in his tone made my lips twitch even as I did my best to ignore the smell of whatever water we stood in.

"Fuck you," I growled.

"No thanks. I'm a little too busy for that."

With a grunt, East shut off the water, and we both stood back, hands on our hips as we stared at the mess of this basement.

East let out a sigh. "I'm not going to have to turn the water off for the whole property, but I'm glad that we don't have tenants in this particular cabin."

I nodded tightly and held back a sigh. "This is probably why there aren't basements in Texas. Because everything seems to go wrong in these things."

"I'm pretty sure this is a storm shelter, or at least a tornado one. Not quite sure as it's one of the only basements in the area."

"It was probably the only one that they had the energy to make back in the day. Considering this whole place is built over clay and limestone."

East nodded, looked around. "I'll start the

cleanup with this water, and we'll look to see what we can do with the pipes."

I pinched the bridge of my nose. "I don't want to have to replace the plumbing for this whole place."

"At least it's not the villa itself, or the farmhouse, or the winery. Just a single cabin."

I glared at my younger brother, then reached out and knocked on a wooden pillar. "Shut your mouth. Don't say things like that to me. We are just now getting our feet under us."

East shrugged. "It's the truth, though. However much you weigh it, it could have been worse."

I pinched the bridge of my nose. "Jesus Christ. You were in the military for how long? A Wilder your entire life, and you say things like that? When the hell did you lose that superstition bone?"

"About the time that my Humvee was blown up, and when Evan's was, Everett's too. Hell, about the time that you almost fell out of the sky in your plane. Or when Elliot was nearly shot to death trying to help one of his men. So, yes, I pretty much lost all superstition when trying to toe the line ended up in near death and maiming."

I met my brother's gaze, that familiar pang thinking about all that we had lost and almost lost over the past few years.

East muttered under his breath, shaking his head. "And I sound more and more like Evan these days rather than myself."

I squeezed his shoulder and let out a breath, thinking of our brother who grunted more than spoke these days. "It's okay. We've been through a lot. But we're here."

Somehow, we were here. I wasn't quite sure if we had made the right decision about two years ago when we had formed this plan, or rather *I* had formed this plan, but there was no going back. We were in it, and we were going to have to find a way to make it work, flooded former tornado shelters and all.

East sighed. "I'll work on this now. Then I'll head on over to the main house. I have a few things to work on there."

"You know, we can hire you help. I know we had all the contractors and everything to work with us for some of the rebuilds and rehabs, but we can hire someone else for you on a day-to-day basis."

My brother shook his head. "We may be able to afford it, but I'd rather save that for a rainy day. Because when it rains, it pours here, and flash flooding is a major threat in this part of Texas." He winked as he said it, mixing his metaphors, and I just shook my head.

"You just let me know if you need it."

"You're the CEO, brother of mine, not the CFO. That's Everett."

"True, but we did talk about it so we can work on it." I paused, thinking about what other expenses might show up. "And what do you need to do with the villa?"

The villa was the main house where most things happened on the property. It contained the lobby, library, and atrium. My apartment was also on the top floor, so I could be there for emergencies. Our innkeeper lived on the other side of the house, but I was in the main loft because this was my project, my baby.

My other brothers, all five of them, lived in cabins on the property. We lived together, worked together, ate together, and fought together. We were the Wilder brothers. It was what we did.

I had left to join the Air Force at seventeen, having graduated early, leaving behind my kid brothers and sister. After nearly twenty years of doing what we needed to in order to survive, we hadn't spent as much time with one another as I would have liked. We hadn't been stationed together, so we hadn't seen one another for longer than holidays or in passing.

But now we were together. At least most of us. So I was going to make this work, even if it killed me.

East finally answered my question. "I just have to fix a door that's a little too squeaky in one of the guestrooms. Not a big deal."

I raised a brow. "That's it?"

"It's one of the many things on my list. Thankfully, this place is big enough that I always have something to do. It's an unending list. And that the winery has its own team to work on all of that shit, because I'm not in the mood to learn to deal with any of the complicated machinery that comes with that world."

I snorted. "Honestly, same. I'm glad there are people that know what the fuck they're doing when it comes to wine making so that didn't have to be the two of us."

I left my brother to this job, knowing he liked time on his own, just like the rest of us did, and went to dry my boots. I was working by myself for most of the day, in interviews and other "boss business," as Elliot called it, so I had to focus and get clean.

I wasn't in the mood to deal with interviews, but

it was part of my job. We had to fill positions that hadn't been working out over the past year, some more than others.

Wilder Retreat was a place that hadn't been even a spark in my mind my entire life. No, I had been too busy being a career military man—getting in my twenty, moving up the ranks, and ending up as a Lieutenant Colonel before I got out. I had been a commander of a squadron, and yet, it felt like I didn't know how to command where I was now.

When my sister Eliza had lost her husband when he was on deployment, it had been the last domino to fall in the Wilder brothers' military career. I had been ready to get out with twenty years in, knowing I needed a career outside of being a Lieutenant Colonel. I wasn't even forty yet, and the term retirement was a misnomer, but that's what happened when it came to my former job.

East had been getting out around that time for reasons of his own, and then Evan had been forced to. I rubbed my hand over my chest, that familiar pain, remembering the phone call from one of Evan's commanders when Evan had been hurt.

I thought I'd lost my baby brother then, and we nearly had. Everett had gotten hurt too, and Elijah and Elliot had needed out for their own reasons.

Losing our baby sister's husband had just pushed us forward.

Finding out that Eliza's husband had been a cheating asshole had just cemented the fact that we needed to spend more time together as a family so we could be there for one another.

In retrospect, it would have been nice if Eliza would have been able to come down to Texas with us, to our suburb outside of San Antonio. Only, she had fallen in love again, with a man with a big family and a good heart up in Fort Collins, Colorado. She was still up there and traveled down enough that we actually got to get to know our sister again.

It was weird to think that, after so many years of always seeing each other in passing or through video calls, most of us were here, opening up a business. And all because I had been losing my mind.

Wilder Retreat and Winery was a villa and wedding venue outside of San Antonio. We were in hill country, at least what passed for hill country in South Texas, and the place had been owned by a former Air Force General who had wanted to retire and sell the place, since his kid didn't want it.

It was a large spread that used to be a ranch back in the day, nearly one hundred acres that the original owners had taken from a working ranch, and instead of making it a dude ranch or something similar, like others did around here, they'd added a winery using local help. We were close enough to Fredericksburg that it made sense in terms of the soil and weather. They had been able to add on additions, so it wasn't just the winery. Someone could come for the day for a winery tour or even a retreat tour, but most people came for the weekend or for a whole week. There were cabins and a farmhouse where we held weddings, dances, or other events. We had some chickens and ducks that gave us eggs, and goats that seemed to have a mind of their own and provided milk for cheese. Then there was the main annex, which housed all the equipment for the retreat villa.

The winery had its own section of buildings, and it was far bigger than anything I would have ever thought that we could handle. But, between the six of us, we did.

And the only reason we could even afford it, because one didn't afford something like this on a military salary, even with a decent retirement plan, was because of our uncles.

Our uncles, Edward and Edmond Wilder, had owned Wilder Wines down in Napa, California, for years. They had done well for themselves, and when we had been kids, we had gone out to visit. Evan had been the one that had clung to it and had been interested in wine making before he had changed his mind and gone into the military like the rest of us.

That was why Evan was in charge of the winery itself now. Because he knew what he was doing, even if he'd growled and said he didn't. Either way though, the place was huge, had multiple working parts at all times, and we had a staff that needed us. But when the uncles had died, they had left the money from the sale of the winery to us in equal parts. Eliza had taken hers to invest for her future children, and the rest of us had pooled our money together to buy this place and make it ours. A lot of the staff from the old owner had stayed, but some had left as well. Because they didn't want new owners who had no idea what they were doing, or they just retired. Either way, we were over a year in and doing okay.

Except for two positions that made me want to groan.

I had an interview with who would be our third wedding planner since we started this. The main component of the retreat was to have an actual wedding venue. To be able to host parties, and not just wine tours. Elliot was our major event planner that helped with our yearly and seasonal minute details, but he didn't want anything to do with the actual weddings. That was a whole other skill set, and so we wanted a wedding planner. We had gone through two wedding planners now, and we needed to hire a third. The first one had lied on her résumé, had given references that were her friends who had lied and had even created websites that were all fabrication, all so she could get into the business. Which, I understood, getting into the business is one thing. However, lying was another. Plus, we needed someone with actual experience because we didn't have any ourselves. We were going out on a limb here with this whole retreat business, and it was all because I had the harebrained idea of getting our family to work together, get along, and get to know one another. I wanted us to have a future, to be our own bosses.

And it was so far over my head that I knew that if I didn't get reliable help, we were going to fail.

Later, I had a meeting with that potential wedding planner. But first, I had to see what the fuck that smell was coming from the main kitchen in the villa.

The second wedding planner we hired was a guy with great and *true* references, one who was good at his job but hated everything to do with my brothers and me. He had hated the idea of the retreat and how rustic it was, even though we were in fucking South Texas. Yes, the buildings look slightly European because that was the theme that the original owners had gone for. Still, the guy had hated us, hadn't listened to us, and had called us white trash before he had walked away, jumped into his convertible, and sped off down the road, leaving us without help. He had been rude to our guests, and now Elliot was the one having to plan weddings for the past three weeks. My brother was going to strangle me soon if we didn't hire someone. And this person was going to be our last hope. As soon as she showed up, that was.

I looked down on my watch and tried to plan the rest of my day. I had thirty minutes to figure out what the hell was going on in the kitchen, and then I had to go to the meeting.

I nodded at a few guests who were sipping wine and eating a cheese plate and then at our innkeeper, Naomi. Naomi's honey-brown hair was cut in an angled bob that lit her face, and she grinned at me.

"Hello there, Boss Man," she whispered. "You might need to go to the kitchen."

"Do I want to know?" I asked with a grumble.

"I'm not sure. But I am going to go check in our next guest, and then Elliott needs to meet with the Henderson couple."

"He'll be there." I didn't say that Elliot would rather chew off his own arm rather than deal with this, considering we had a family event coming in, one that Elliot was on target with planning. The wedding for next year was an important one, so we needed to work on it.

Naomi was a fantastic innkeeper, far more organized than any of us—and that was saying something since my brothers and I knew our way around schedules, to-do lists, and spreadsheets. Naomi was personable, smiled, and kept us on our toes.

Without her, I knew we wouldn't be able to do this. Hell, without Amos, our vineyard manager, I knew that Evan and Elijah wouldn't be able to handle the winery as they did. Naomi and Amos had come with the place when we had bought it, and I would be forever grateful that they had decided to stay on.

I gave Naomi another nod, then headed back to the kitchen and nearly walked right back out.

Tony stood there, a scowl on his face and his hands on his hips. "I don't understand what the fuck is wrong with this oven."

"What's going on?" I asked as Everett stood by Tony. Everett was my quiet brother with usually a small smile on his face, only right then it looked like he was ready to scream.

I didn't know why Everett was even there since he was part responsible for the financials side of the company and usually worked with Elliot these days. Maybe he had come to the kitchen after the smell of burning as I had after Naomi's prodding.

Tony threw his hands in the air. "What's going on? This stove is a piece of shit. All of it is a piece of shit. I'm tired of this rustic place. I thought I would be coming to a Michelin star restaurant. To be my own chef. Instead, I have to make English breakfasts and pancakes with bananas. I might as well be at a bed and breakfast."

I pinched the bridge of my nose. "We're an inn, not a bed and breakfast."

"But I serve breakfast. That's all I do these days. That and cheese platters. Nobody comes for dinner. Nobody comes for lunch."

That was a lie. Tony worked for the winery and the retreat itself and served all the meals. But Tony wanted to go crazy with the menu, to try new and fantastical items that just weren't going to work here.

And I had a feeling I was going to throw up if I wasn't careful.

"I quit," Tony snapped, and I knew right then, it was done for. I was done.

"You can't quit," I growled while Everett held back a sigh.

"Yes, I can. I'm done. I'm done with you and this ranch. You're not cowboys. You're not even Texans. You're just people moving in on our territory." And with that, Tony stomped away, throwing his chef's apron on the ground.

I was thankful that the kitchen was on the other side of the library and front area, where most of the guests were if they weren't out on one of the tours of the area and city that Elliott had arranged for them. That was the whole point of this retreat. They could come visit, and could relax, or we could set them up on a tour of downtown San Antonio, or Canyon Lake, or any of the other places that were nearby.

And yet, Tony had just thrown a wrench into all of that. I didn't know what was worse, the smell of burning, Tony leaving, the water in the basement that wasn't truly a basement, or the fact that I was going to smell like charred food and wet jeans when I went to go meet this wedding planner.

"You're going to need to hire a new cook," Everett whispered.

I looked at my brother, at the man who did his best to make sure we didn't go bankrupt, and I wanted to just grumble. "I figured."

"I can help for now, but you know I'm only part-time. I can't stay away from my twins for too long," Sandy said as she came forward to take the pan off the stove. "I wish I could do full time, but this is all I can do for now."

Sandy had come back from maternity leave after we had already opened the retreat. She had been on with the former owners and was brilliant. But she had a right to be a mom and not want to work full time. I understood that, and I knew that Sandy didn't want to handle a whole kitchen by herself. She liked her position as a sous chef.

I was going to have to figure out what to do. Again.

"I'll get it done," I said while rubbing my temples.

"You know what we need to do," Everett whispered, and I shook my head.

"He'll kill us."

"Maybe, but it'll be worth it in the end. And speaking of, don't you have that interview soon? Or do you want me to take it?" His gaze tracked to my jeans.

I shook my head. "No, help Sandy."

Everett winced. "Just because I know how to slice an onion, it doesn't mean I'm good at cooking."

"I'm sorry, did you just say you could slice an onion? Get to it," Sandy put in with a smile, pointing at the sink. "Wash those hands."

"I cannot believe I just said that out loud. I just stepped right into it," Everett said with a sigh. "Go to the interview. You know what to ask."

"I do. And I hope we don't get screwed this time."

"You know, if we're lucky, we'll get someone as good as Roy's wedding planner, or at least that woman that we met. You know who she is." Everett grinned like a cat with the canary.

I narrowed my eyes. "Don't bring her up."

"Oh, I can't help it. A single dance, and you were drawn to her."

"What dance? You know what? No, I don't have time. We have to work on lunch and dinner. Tell me while you work," Sandy added with a wink.

Everett leaned toward her as he washed his hands. "Well, you see, there was this dance, and he met the perfect woman, and then she got engaged."

Sandy's eyes widened. "Engaged? How did that happen? She was dating someone else?" she asked as she looked at me.

I pinched the bridge of my nose. "It was at Roy's place when we were looking at the venue to see if we wanted to buy the retreat here." I sighed, I knew if I just let it all out, she would move on from this conversation, and I would never have to deal with it again. "Somehow, I ended up at a wedding there, caught the garter. This woman caught the bouquet, and she happened to be the wedding planner. We danced, we laughed, and as she walked away, her boyfriend got down on one knee and proposed."

"No way!" She leaned forward with a fierce look on her face, her eyes bright. "What did she say?"

"I have no clue. I left." I ignored whatever feeling might want to show up at that thought. Everett gave me a glance, and I shook my head. "Enough of that. Yes, the wedding that she did was great, but I honestly have no idea who she is, and she has a job. She doesn't need to work here." And I didn't know what I would do if I saw her again or had to work with her. There had been such an intense connection that I knew it would be awkward as hell. But thankfully, she had her own business and wasn't going to come to the Wilder Retreat for a job.

I left Sandy and Everett on their own, knowing that they were capable, at least for now. And I knew who we would have to hire if she said yes, and if my other brother didn't kill me first.

I washed my hands in the sink on the way out, grateful that at least I looked somewhat decent, if not a little disheveled, and made my way out front, hoping that the wedding planner who came in through the doors would be the one that would stick. Because we needed some good luck. After the day we've had, we needed some good luck.

I turned the corner and nearly tripped over my feet.

Because, of course, fate was this way.

It was her.

Of all the wedding planners from all the wedding venues, it was her.

In the mood to read another family saga? Meet the Wilder Brothers in One Way Back to Me!

FROM BITTERSWEET PROMISES

LEIF

"Not only did you convince me to somehow go on a blind date, it became a double date. How on earth did you work this magic on me, cousin?" I asked Lake as she leaned against the pillar just inside the restaurant.

Lake grinned at me, her dark hair pulled away from her face. She had on this swingy black dress and looked as if she were excited, anxious, nervous, and happy all at the same time. Considering she was bouncing on her toes when usually Lake was calm, cool, and collected, was saying something. "I asked, and you said yes. Because you love me."

"I might love you because we're family, but I still think we're making a mistake." I shook my head and pulled at my shirt sleeves. Lake had somehow convinced me to wear a button-up shirt tucked into gray pants, I even had on shiny shoes. I looked like a damn banker. But if that's what Lake wanted, that's what I would do.

Lake might technically be my cousin, even though we weren't blood-related, but we were more like brother and sister than any of my other cousins.

I had siblings, as did Lake, but with the generational gap, we were at least a decade older than all of our other cousins. That meant, despite the fact that we had lived over an hour apart for most of our lives, we'd grown up more like siblings.

I loved my three younger siblings and talked to them daily. Unlike some blended families, they *were* my brothers and sister and not like strangers or distant family members. I didn't feel a disconnect from the three of them, but Lake was still closer to me.

Probably because we were either heading into our thirties or already there, where most of our other cousins were either just now in their early twenties or still teenagers in high school. With how big we Montgomerys were as a family, it made sense that there would be such a widespread age group. That meant that Lake and I were best friends, cousins, practically siblings, and sometimes the banes of each other's existences.

We were also business owners and partners and saw each other too often these days. That was probably why she convinced me to go on a blind double date. But she had been out with Zach before. I, however, had never met May. Lake had some connection with her that I wasn't sure about, and for some reason Lake's date had said yes to this double date.

And, in the complicated way of family, I had agreed to it. I must have been tired. Or perhaps I'd had too many beers. Because I didn't do blind dates, and recently, I didn't do dates at all.

Lake scanned her phone, then looked up at me, all innocence in her smart gaze. "You shouldn't have told me you wanted to settle down in your old age."

I narrowed my eyes. "I'm still in my early thirties, jerk. Stop calling me old."

"I shouldn't call you old since you're only a few years older than me." She fluttered her eyelashes and I flipped her off, ignoring the stare from the older woman next to me. Though I was a tattoo artist, I didn't have many visible tattoos. Most of mine were on my back and legs, hidden from the world unless I wanted to show them. I hadn't figured out what I wanted on my arms beyond a few small pieces on my wrists and upper shoulders. And since tattoos were permanent, I was taking my time. If a client needed to see my skin with ink to feel comfortable, I'd show them my back. My body was a canvas, so I did what I could to set people at ease.

But I still had the eyebrow piercing and had recently taken out my nose ring. I didn't look too scary for most people. But apparently, flipping off a woman, growling, and cursing a time or two in front of strangers probably made me appear too close to the dark side.

"Yes, I want to settle down, but this will be awkward, won't it? Where the two of us are strangers, and the two of you aren't?" I wanted a life, a future, and yeah, one day to settle down with someone. I just didn't know why I'd mentioned it to Lake in the first place.

"If it helps, May doesn't know Zach, either. So it's a group of strangers, except I know everybody." She clapped her hands together and did her version of an evil laugh, and I just shook my head.

"Considering what you do for a living and how you like to manipulate things in your way, this makes sense. Are you going to be adding a match-making company to your conglomerate?"

Lake just fluttered her eyelashes again and laughed. Lake owned a small tech company that made a shit ton of money over the past couple of years. And because she was brilliant at what she did, innovative, and liked pushing money towards women-owned businesses, she owned more than one company at this point and was an investor in mine. I wouldn't be surprised if she found a way to open up a women-owned matchmaking company right here in town.

"It might be fun. I can call it Montgomery Links." Her eyes went wide. "Oh, my God. I have to write that down." She pulled out her phone, began to take notes, and I pinched the bridge of my nose.

"You know I trust you with my actual life, but I don't know if I trust you with my dating life."

Lake tossed her hair behind her shoulder as she continued to type. "Shut up. You love me. And once I finish setting you up, the rest of the family's next."

"Oh, really? You're going to get Daisy and Noah next?" I asked, speaking of two more of our cousins.

"Maybe. Of course, Sebastian's the only one of the younger group that seems to have a serious girlfriend."

I nodded, speaking of our other familial business partner. Sebastian was still a teenager, though in college. He had wanted to open up Montgomery Ink Legacy with me, the full title of our company. There was a legacy to it, and Sebastian had wanted in. So, though he didn't work there full-time, he was putting his future towards us. And in the ways of young love, he and his girlfriend had been together since middle school. The fact that my younger cousin was better at relationships than I was didn't make me feel great. But I was going to ignore that.

"You're not going to start up a matchmaking service, are you? Or maybe an app?"

"Dating apps are ridiculous these days, they practically want you to invest in coins to bid on dates, and that's not something I'm in the mood for. But maybe there's something I can try. I'll add it to my list."

Lake's list of inventions and tech was notorious, and knowing the brilliance of my cousin, she would one day rule the world and might eventually cross everything off that list.

"Oh, here's Zach." Lake's face brightened immediately, and she smiled up at a man with dark hair, piercing gray eyes, and an actual dimple on his cheek.

Tonight was not only about my blind date, but me getting the lay of the land when it came to Zach.

I was the first step into meeting the family. Oh, if Zach passed my gauntlet, he would meet the rest of the Montgomerys, and we were mighty. All one hundred of us.

"Zach, you're here." Lake's voice went soft, and she went on her tiptoes even in her high heels as Zach pressed a soft kiss to her lips.

"Of course, I'm here. And you're early, as usual."

Lake blushed and ducked her head. "Well, you know me. I like to be early because being on time is late," she said at the same time I did, mumbling under my breath. It was a familiar refrain when it came to us.

"Zach, good to meet you," I said, holding out my hand.

The other man gripped it firmly and shook. "Nice to meet you too, Leif. I know you might be the one on a blind date soon, but I'm nervous."

I chuckled, shaking my head. "Yeah, I'm pretty nervous too. Though I'm grateful that Lake's trying to look out for me."

My cousin laughed softly. "You totally were not saying that a few minutes ago, but be suave and sophisticated now. Or just be yourself, May's on her way."

I met Zach's gaze and we both rolled our eyes.

When I turned toward the door, I saw a woman of average height, with black straight hair, green eyes, and a sweet smile. I didn't know much about May, other than Lake knew her and liked her. If I was going to start dating again after taking time off to get the rest of my life together, I might as well start with someone that one of my best friends liked.

"May, I'm so glad that you're here," Lake said as she hugged the other woman tightly.

As Lake began to bounce on her heels, I realized that my cousin's cool, calm, and collected exterior was only for work. She was bouncing and happy when it came to her friends or when she was nervous. I knew that, of course, but I had forgotten how she had turned into the mogul that she was. It was good to see her relaxed and happy.

Now I just needed to figure out how to do that for myself.

May stood in front of me, and I felt like I was starting middle school all over again. A new school, a new life, and a past that didn't make much sense to anyone else.

I swallowed hard and nodded, not putting out my hand to shake, thinking that would be weird, but I also didn't want to hug her. I didn't even know this woman. Why was everything so awkward? Instead, I lifted my chin. "Hello, May. It's nice to meet you. Lake says only good things."

There, smooth. Not really. Zach began to move out of frame, with Lake at his side as the two went to speak to the hostess, leaving May and me alone.

This wasn't going to be awkward at all.

The woman just smiled at me, her eyes wide. "It's nice to meet you, too. And Lake does speak highly of you. Also, this is very awkward, so I'm so sorry if I say something stupid. I know that your cousin said that I should be set up with you which is great but I'm not great at blind dates and apparently this is a double date and now I'm going to stop talking." She said the words so quickly they all ran into one breath.

I shook my head and laughed. "We're on the same page there."

"Okay, good. It's nice to meet you, Leif Montgomery."

"And it's nice to meet you too, May."

We made our way to Lake and Zach, who had gotten our table, and we all sat down, talking about work and other things. May was in child life development, taught online classes, and was also a nanny.

"I'm actually about to start with a new family

soon. I'm excited. I know that being a nanny isn't something that most people strive for, or at least that's what they tell you, but I love being able to work with children and be the person that is there when a single parent or even both parents are out in the workforce, trying to do everything."

I nodded, taking a sip of my beer. "I get you completely. With how my parents worked, I was lucky that they were able to get childcare within the buildings. Since they each owned their own businesses, they made it work. But my family worked long hours, and that's why I ended up being the babysitter a lot of the times when childcare wasn't an option." I cleared my throat. "I'm a lot older than a lot of my cousins," I added.

"Both of us are, but I'm glad that you only said yourself," Lake said, grinning. She leaned into Zach as she spoke, the four of us in a horseshoe-shaped booth. That gave May and me space since this was a first date and still awkward as hell, and so Lake and Zach could cuddle. Not that that was something I needed to be a part of.

"Oh, I'm glad that you didn't judge. The last few dates that I've been on they always gave me weird looks because I think they expected a nanny to be this old crone or someone that's looking for a different job." She shrugged and continued. "When I eventually get married and maybe even start a family, I want to continue my job. I like being there to help another family achieve their goals. And I can't believe I just said start a family on my first date. And that I mentioned that I've been on a few other dates." She let out a breath. "I'm notoriously bad at dating. Like, the worst. Just warning you."

I laughed, shaking my head. "I'm rusty at it, so don't worry." And even though I said that, I had a feeling that May felt no spark towards me, and I didn't feel anything towards her. She was nice and pleasant, and I could probably consider her a friend one day. But there wasn't any spark. May's eyes weren't dancing. She wasn't leaning forward, trying to touch my hand across the table. We were just sitting there casually, enjoying a really good steak, as Lake and Zach enjoyed their date.

By the end of dinner, I didn't want dessert, and neither did May, so we said goodbye to the other couple, who decided to stay. I walked May to her car, ignoring Lake's warning look, but I didn't know what exactly she was warning me about.

"Thanks for dinner," May said. "I could have paid. I know this is a blind date and all that, but you didn't have to pay."

I shook my head. "I paid for the four of us because I wanted to be nice. I'll make Lake pay next time."

May beamed. "Yes, I like that. You guys are a good family."

"Anyway," I said, clearing my throat as I stuck my hands in my pockets. "I guess I'll see you around."

May just looked at me, threw her head back, and laughed. "You're right. You are rusty at this."

"Sorry." Heat flushed my skin, and I resisted the urge to tug on my eyebrow ring.

"It's okay. No spark. I'm used to it. I don't spark well."

"May, I'm sorry." I cringed. "It's not you."

"Oh, God, please don't say that. 'It's not you. It's me. You're working on yourself. You're just so busy with work.' I've heard it all."

"Seriously?" I asked. May was hot. Nice, but there just wasn't a spark.

She shrugged. "It's okay. I'll probably see you around sometime because I am friends with Lake. However, I am perfectly fine having this be our one and only. You'll find your person. It's okay that it's not me." And with that, she got in the car and left, leaving me standing there.

Well then. Tonight wasn't horrible, but it wasn't great. I got in my car, and instead of heading home where I'd be alone, watching something on some streaming service while I drank a beer and pretended that I knew what I was doing with my life, I headed into Montgomery Ink Legacy.

We were the third branch of the company and the first owned by our generation. Montgomery Ink was the tattoo shop in downtown Denver. While there were open spots for some walk-ins and special circumstances, my father, aunt, and their team had years' worth of waiting lists. They worked their asses off and made sure to get in everybody that they could, but people wanted Austin Montgomery's art. Same with my aunt, Maya.

There was another tattoo shop down in Colorado Springs, owned by my parents' cousins, who I just called aunt and uncle because we were close enough that using real titles for everybody got confusing. Montgomery Ink Too was thriving down there, and they had waiting lists as well. My family could have opened more shops and gone nationwide, even global if they wanted to, but they liked keeping it how it was, in the family and those connected.

We were a branch, but our own in the making. I had gone into business with Lake, of course, and Sebastian, when he was ready, as well as Nick. Nick was my best friend. I had known him for ages, and he had wanted to be part of something as well. He might not be a Montgomery by name, but he had eaten over at my family's house enough times throughout the years that he was practically a Montgomery. And he had invested in the company as well, and so now we were nearly a year into owning the shop and trying not to fail.

I pulled into the parking lot, grateful it was still open since we didn't close until nine most nights, and greeted Nick, who was still working.

Sebastian was in the back, going over sketches with a client, and I nodded at him. He might be eighteen, but he was still in training, an apprentice, and was working his ass off to learn.

"Date sucked then?" Sebastian asked, and Nick just rolled his eyes and went back to work on a client's wrist.

"I don't want to talk about it," I groaned.

The rest of the staff was off since Nick would close up on his own. Sebastian was just there since he didn't have homework or a date with Marley.

"Was she hot at least?" Sebastian asked, and the

client, a woman in her sixties, bopped him on the head with her bag gently.

"Sebastian Montgomery. Be nice."

Sebastian blushed. "Sorry, Mrs. Anderson."

I looked over at the woman and grinned. "Hi, Mrs. Anderson. It's nice to see you out of the classroom."

She narrowed her eyes at me, even though they filled with laughter. "I needed my next Jane Austen tattoo, thank you very much," the older woman said as she went back to working with Sebastian. She had been my and then Sebastian's English teacher. The fact that she was on her fifth tattoo with some literary quote told me that I had been damn lucky in most of my teachers growing up.

She was kick-ass, and I had a feeling that she would let Sebastian do the tattoo for her rather than just have him work on the design with me as we did for most of the people who came in. He had learned under my father and was working under me now. It was strange to think that he wasn't a little kid anymore. But he was in a long-term relationship, kicking ass in college, and knew what he wanted to do with his life.

I might know what I want to do with my work life, but everything else seemed a little off.

"So it didn't work out?" Nick asked as he walked up to the front desk with the clients after going over aftercare.

"Not really," I said, looking down at my phone.

The client, a woman in her mid-twenties with bright pink hair, a lip ring, and kind eyes, leaned over the desk to look at me.

"You'll find someone, Leif. Don't worry."

I looked at our regular and shook my head. "Thanks, Kim. Too bad that you don't swing this way."

I winked as I said it, a familiar refrain from both of us.

Kim was married to a woman named Sonya, and the two of them were happy and working on in vitro with donated sperm for their first kid.

"Hey, I'm sorry too that I'm a lesbian. I'll never know what it means to have Leif Montgomery. Or any Montgomery, since I found my love far too quickly. I mean, what am I ever going to do not knowing the love of a Montgomery?"

Mrs. Anderson chuckled from her chair, Sebastian held back a snort, and I just looked at Nick, who rolled his eyes and helped Kim out of the place.

I was tired, but it was okay. The date wasn't all

bad. May was nice. But it felt like I didn't have much right then.

And then Nick sat in front of me, scowled, and I realized that I did have something. I had my friends and my family. I didn't need much more.

"So, you and May didn't work out?"

I raised a brow. "You knew her name? Did I tell you that?"

Nick shook his head. "Lake did."

That made sense, considering the two of them spoke as much as we did. "So, was it your idea to set me up on a blind date?"

"Fuck no. That was all Lake. I just do what she says. Like we all do."

I sighed and went through my appointments for the next day. "We're busy for the next month. That's good, right?" I asked.

"You're the business genius here. I just play with ink. But yes, that's good. Now, don't let your cousin set you up any more dates. Find them for yourself. You know what you're doing."

"So says the man who dates less than me."

"That's what you think. I'm more private about it. As it should be." I flipped him off as he stood up, then he gestured towards a stack of bills in the corner. "You have a few personal things that made their way here. Don't want you to miss out on them before you head home."

"Thanks, bro."

"No problem. I'm going to help Sebastian with his consult, and then I'll clean up. You should head home. Though you're doing it alone, so I feel sorry for you."

"Fuck you," I called out.

"Fuck you, too."

"Boys," Mrs. Anderson said, in that familiar English teacher refrain, and both Nick and I cringed before saying, "Sorry," simultaneously.

Sebastian snickered, then went back to work, and I headed towards the edge of the counter, picking up the stack of papers. Most were bills, some were random papers that needed to be filed or looked over. Some were just junk mail. But there was one letter, written in block print that didn't look familiar. Chills went up my spine and I opened it, wondering what the fuck this was. Maybe it was someone asking to buy my house. I got a lot of hand-written letters for that, but I didn't think this was going to be that. I swallowed hard, slid open the paper, and froze.

"I'll find you, boy. Oops. Looks like I already did. Be waiting. I know you miss me."

I let the paper hit the top of the counter and swallowed hard, trying to remain cool so I didn't worry anyone else.

I didn't know exactly who that was from, but I had a horrible feeling that they wouldn't wait long to tell me.

Read the rest in Bittersweet Promises!
OUT NOW!

ALSO FROM CARRIE ANN RYAN

The Montgomery Ink Legacy Series:

Book 1: Bittersweet Promises (Leif & Brooke)

Book 2: At First Meet (Nick & Lake)

Book 2.5: Happily Ever Never (May & Leo)

Book 3: Longtime Crush (Sebastian & Raven)

Book 4: Best Friend Temptation (Noah, Ford, and Greer)

Book 4.5: Happily Ever Maybe (Jennifer & Gus)

Book 5: Last First Kiss (Daisy & Hugh)

Book 6: His Second Chance (Kane & Phoebe)

Book 7: One Night with You (Kingston & Claire)

Book 8: Accidentally Forever (Crew & Aria)

Book 9: Last Chance Seduction (Lexington & Mercy)

Book 10: Kiss Me Forever (Brooklyn & Reece)

Book 11: His Guilty Pleasure (Dash & Aly)

The Cage Family

Book 1: The Forever Rule (Aston & Blakely)

Book 2: An Unexpected Everything (Isabella & Weston)

Book 3: If You Were Mine (Dorian & Harper)

Book 4: One Quick Obsession (Hudson & Scarlett)

Book 5: Pretend it's Forever (???? & ????)

Ashford Creek

Book 1: Legacy (Callum & Felicity)

Book 2: Crossroads (Bohdi & Keira)

Book 3: Westward (Atlas & Elizabeth)

Clover Lake

Book 1: Always a Fake Bridesmaid (Livvy & Ewan)

Book 2: Accidental Runaway Groom (Jamie & Sharp)

The Wilder Brothers Series:

Book 1: One Way Back to Me (Eli & Alexis)

Book 2: Always the One for Me (Evan & Kendall)

Book 3: The Path to You (Everett & Bethany)

Book 4: Coming Home for Us (Elijah & Maddie)

Book 5: Stay Here With Me (East & Lark)

Book 6: Finding the Road to Us (Elliot, Trace, and Sidney)

Book 7: Moments for You (Ridge & Aurora)

Book 7.5: A Wilder Wedding (Amos & Naomi)

Book 8: Forever For Us (Wyatt & Ava)

Book 9: Pieces of Me (Gabriel & Briar)

Book 10: Endlessly Yours (Brooks & Rory)

The Falling for the Cassidy Brothers Series:

Book 1: Good Time Boyfriend (Heath & Devney)

Book 2: Last Minute Fiancé (Luca & Addison)

Book 3: Second Chance Husband (August & Paisley)

Montgomery Ink Denver:

Book 0.5: <u>Ink Inspired</u> (Shep & Shea)

Book 0.6: <u>Ink Reunited</u> (Sassy, Rare, and Ian)

Book 1: <u>Delicate Ink</u> (Austin & Sierra)

Book 1.5: <u>Forever Ink</u> (Callie & Morgan)

Book 2: <u>Tempting Boundaries</u> (Decker and Miranda)

Book 3: <u>Harder than Words</u> (Meghan & Luc)

Book 3.5: <u>Finally Found You</u> (Mason & Presley)

Book 4: <u>Written in Ink</u> (Griffin & Autumn)

Book 4.5: <u>Hidden Ink</u> (Hailey & Sloane)

Book 5: <u>Ink Enduring</u> (Maya, Jake, and Border)

Book 6: <u>Ink Exposed</u> (Alex & Tabby)

Book 6.5: <u>Adoring Ink</u> (Holly & Brody)

Book 6.6: <u>Love, Honor, & Ink</u> (Arianna & Harper)

Book 7: <u>Inked Expressions</u> (Storm & Everly)

Book 7.3: <u>Dropout</u> (Grayson & Kate)

Book 7.5: <u>Executive Ink</u> (Jax & Ashlynn)

Book 8: <u>Inked Memories</u> (Wes & Jillian)

Book 8.5: <u>Inked Nights</u> (Derek & Olivia)

Book 8.7: <u>Second Chance Ink</u> (Brandon & Lauren)

Book 8.5: Montgomery Midnight Kisses (Alex & Tabby Bonus(

Bonus: Inked Kingdom (Stone & Sarina)

Montgomery Ink: Colorado Springs

Book 1: Fallen Ink (Adrienne & Mace)

Book 2: Restless Ink (Thea & Dimitri)

Book 2.5: Ashes to Ink (Abby & Ryan)

Book 3: Jagged Ink (Roxie & Carter)

Book 3.5: Ink by Numbers (Landon & Kaylee)

The Montgomery Ink: Boulder Series:

Book 1: Wrapped in Ink (Liam & Arden)

Book 2: Sated in Ink (Ethan, Lincoln, and Holland)

Book 3: Embraced in Ink (Bristol & Marcus)

Book 3: Moments in Ink (Zia & Meredith)

Book 4: Seduced in Ink (Aaron & Madison)

Book 4.5: Captured in Ink (Julia, Ronin, & Kincaid)

Book 4.7: Inked Fantasy (Secret ??)

Book 4.8: A Very Montgomery Christmas (The Entire Boulder Family)

The Montgomery Ink: Fort Collins Series:

Book 1: Inked Persuasion (Jacob & Annabelle)

Book 2: Inked Obsession (Beckett & Eliza)

Book 3: Inked Devotion (Benjamin & Brenna)

Book 3.5: Nothing But Ink (Clay & Riggs)

Book 4: Inked Craving (Lee & Paige)

Book 5: Inked Temptation (Archer & Killian)

The Promise Me Series:

Book 1: Forever Only Once (Cross & Hazel)

Book 2: From That Moment (Prior & Paris)

Book 3: Far From Destined (Macon & Dakota)

Book 4: From Our First (Nate & Myra)

The Whiskey and Lies Series:

Book 1: <u>Whiskey Secrets</u> (Dare & Kenzie)

Book 2: <u>Whiskey Reveals</u> (Fox & Melody)

Book 3: <u>Whiskey Undone</u> (Loch & Ainsley)

The Gallagher Brothers Series:

Book 1: <u>Love Restored</u> (Graham & Blake)

Book 2: <u>Passion Restored</u> (Owen & Liz)

Book 3: <u>Hope Restored</u> (Murphy & Tessa)

The Less Than Series:

Book 1: Breathless With Her (Devin & Erin)

Book 2: Reckless With You (Tucker & Amelia)

Book 3: Shameless With Him (Caleb & Zoey)

The Fractured Connections Series:

Book 1: Breaking Without You (Cameron & Violet)

Book 2: Shouldn't Have You (Brendon & Harmony)

Book 3: Falling With You (Aiden & Sienna)

Book 4: Taken With You (Beckham & Meadow)

The On My Own Series:

Book 0.5: My First Glance

Book 1: My One Night (Dillon & Elise)

Book 2: My Rebound (Pacey & Mackenzie)

Book 3: My Next Play (Miles & Nessa)

Book 4: My Bad Decisions (Tanner & Natalie)

The Ravenwood Coven Series:

Book 1: Dawn Unearthed

Book 2: Dusk Unveiled

Book 3: Evernight Unleashed

The Aspen Pack Series:

Book 1: Etched in Honor

Book 2: Hunted in Darkness

Book 3: Mated in Chaos

Book 4: Harbored in Silence

Book 5: Marked in Flames

The Talon Pack:

Book 1: Tattered Loyalties

Book 2: An Alpha's Choice

Book 3: Mated in Mist

Book 4: Wolf Betrayed

Book 5: Fractured Silence

Book 6: Destiny Disgraced

Book 7: Eternal Mourning

Book 8: Strength Enduring

Book 9: Forever Broken

Book 10: Mated in Darkness

Book 2: <u>Her Warriors' Three Wishes</u>

Book 3: <u>An Unlucky Moon</u>

Book 3.5: <u>His Choice</u>

Book 4: <u>Tangled Innocence</u>

Book 5: <u>Fierce Enchantment</u>

Book 6: <u>An Immortal's Song</u>

Book 7: <u>Prowled Darkness</u>

Book 8: Dante's Circle Reborn

Holiday, Montana Series:

Book 1: <u>Charmed Spirits</u>

Book 2: <u>Santa's Executive</u>

Book 3: <u>Finding Abigail</u>

Book 4: <u>Her Lucky Love</u>

Book 5: Dreams of Ivory

The Branded Pack Series:

(Written with Alexandra Ivy)

Book 1: <u>Stolen and Forgiven</u>

Book 2: <u>Abandoned and Unseen</u>

Book 3: <u>Buried and Shadowed</u>

www.CarrieAnnRyan.com

www.ingramcontent.com/pod-product-compliance
Lightning Source LLC
Chambersburg PA
CBHW010738130726
47899CB00015B/3374